Hearts of Gold

The Bridal Shop

GRACE HITCHCOCK

Published by Valmont House Publishers

GraceHitchcock.com

Names: Hitchcock, Grace, author.

Title: The Bridal Shop / Grace Hitchcock

Other Titles: the bridal shop

Identifiers: 978-1-970675-07-8 Paperback

Subjects: Christian Romantic fiction

All scripture quotations, unless otherwise noted, are taken from the King James Version of the Bible.

Cover design by *Valmont House Publishers*

Editor Ellen Tarver

Author is represented by The Steve Laube Agency

More From Grace Hitchcock:

Aprons and Veils Series:
The Finding of Miss Fairfield
The Pursuit of Miss Parish
The Enchanting of Miss Elliot
The Vanishing of Miss Victoria
The Courting of Miss Cady
The Making of Miss Matthews

Best Laid Plans Series:
To Catch a Coronet
To Kiss a Knight
To Win a Wager

American Royalty Series:
My Dear Miss Dupré
Her Darling Mr. Day
His Delightful Lady Delia

Heiresses of Adventure Series:
Miss Blaire in Blackwell's Island
Miss Wylde in the White City

Novellas:

Hearts of Gold, a Historical Romance Collection

"The Widow of St. Charles Avenue" in Second Chance Brides Collection

He healeth the broken in heart,
and bindeth up their wounds.
PSALM 147:3

CHAPTER ONE

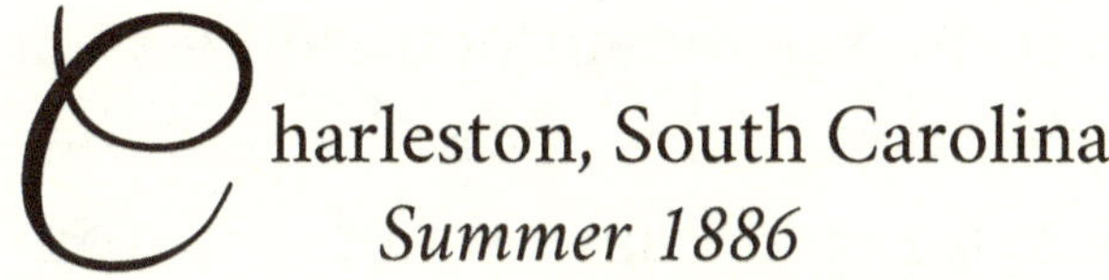harleston, South Carolina

Summer 1886

ALICE TURNER ROLLED the silver thimble between her fingers and thumb as she stepped aside, watching the bride twirl before the bedroom's gilded looking glass.

The bridesmaid's eyes adopted a hungry expression, gazing at Alice's latest masterpiece of ivory satin and tulle. "I've never seen anything quite as beautiful as this wedding gown. What do you think, Constance? Would your mother have approved?"

The bride's skirts stilled as she picked at

the cuff of the gown, causing Alice to stiffen. If Miss Constance Clayton did not approve and word circulated. . . Alice took a tentative step forward, her jaw tensing as she clasped her hands in front of her cream skirts.

"The lacework is unrivaled. I believe Mother would've been pleased." Constance sent Alice an approving nod. "It was a risk engaging a local seamstress for my wedding gown, even someone recommended by such a trusted friend as Mrs. Martin and her daughter, when I could have sent for it from Paris. But my early engagement was not expected, and since my fiancé and I wanted a double wedding with William and Meg, I dared not hope the gown would arrive on time."

Alice nodded at the not-so-subtle reminder that she was only hired because her best friend, Meg, was marrying Constance's brother, William Clayton. She would not squander this chance to break into the elite set, which was why she personally attended to this bride's fitting instead of her assistant.

"Eustace is going to be so pleased." Constance sighed as she ran her hands over the pearl beadwork on the bodice and preened in the looking glass.

Eustace. Alice's heart dipped at the name of her former fiancé. Surely the groom couldn't be *her* Eustace. *Could he?* She despised herself for asking, but she had to know. "Eustace, what a genteel name. He must be from a good family." She paused, waiting for the bride to fill in the surname, but Constance merely nodded, distracted with the demure puffed sleeves, so Alice pressed, "What is his family name? Perhaps I could stitch your initials together on the interior hem to add a touch of sentiment. I would, of course, stitch them with blue thread for your 'something blue' to wear."

"What a lovely idea." Constance turned her back to Alice, motioning for her to unfasten the row of silk buttons. "His name is Eustace Merrick."

Not my Eustace. The relief in her shoulders was short-lived, for she didn't know why she was *still* concerned if he had married or not. It had been five years. Five *long* years since he had broken her heart on those courthouse steps. Her fingers fumbled on the last button.

"It will only take me a moment," she whispered and lowered the gown for the bride to step out. Whisking the dress into the corner of the room where she had her sewing supplies stacked beside a Queen Anne's chair, she set to work on embroidering the initials in neat, tiny stitches in Eustace's favorite color and wondered if it was still his favorite. *Stop it,* she scolded herself.

Since that horrid day nearly five years ago, she had attempted to put him out of her mind for good, but memories of him were spread across Charleston. The park where they had shared their first kiss beneath the swaying Spanish moss of an oak was on her way to Miss Clayton's, the fountain where he had proposed was only a few blocks from her shop on King Street. . .and the courthouse steps where he had broken her heart was a route she avoided altogether.

Forcing herself to set aside the painful memories, she snipped the ends of the thread with her scissors, shook the gown free from any loose threads, and draped it over her arm to display her handiwork to the bride, causing a squeal and an impromptu hug from the generally rigid Constance Clayton.

Miss Hyacinth Castle, the bridesmaid, ran her finger over the neat stiches as she slowly smiled. "What a clever touch. I'm sure your work will draw the attention of many at the wedding. Now, if you'll excuse us, my friend and I need to ready for the bridal luncheon."

"Of course. And if you have need of anything, day or night, just send word to this address, and I'll be there." Alice handed them each her business card, dipped into a curtsy, and gathered her things, making her way back to her bridal shop.

GILES CLAYTON HAD to get out of the office. After dealing with an excessively demanding customer, he needed a breath of fresh air. Taking a stroll down King Street, he breathed deeply, enjoying the warm, humid breeze as it brought him to life even if it was tinged with the scent of the hired carriages' horses. Anything was favorable to sitting with that client for another minute. He stretched his shoulders, wincing at the stiffness that had set in from hours of sitting at his desk. After the thrill of playing in Wimbledon and years of instructing tennis abroad, banking felt positively suffocating. He missed the excitement of the courts, but with his father's impending retirement, he knew it was time for him to step up and become the man his family needed him to be, a tennis champion turned banker.

At the cheer of some boys in one of the alleyways, he paused to find a ratty baseball landing on the sidewalk in front of him and rolling out toward the busy street. Giles squatted down to catch it and keep it from rolling into the street, and a resounding rip and a cool breeze greeted him.

Oh no. He jerked to standing and pulled his jacket low to cover what he could of his exposed undergarment as he kicked the ball to the boys and turned his back to the alley wall, trying to gather himself. There were far too many ladies shopping on King Street for him to simply waltz back into his office for his tennis trousers, and if word got out at work, he would be a laughingstock. He might even be arrested for public indecency before he reached home. He scratched his chin. *And to hail a cab would mean to lift my arm. That can't happen with all these people about. Blast.*

Holding his jacket low, he shuffled out toward King Street again, but spying a gaggle of women coming toward him, Giles ducked back into the shadow of the building and waited until they had passed before peeking out again onto the street. Squinting in the glare of the sun, he caught sight of a wooden sign depicting a thimble and a spool of thread. THIMBLES AND THREADS BRIDAL SHOP. Giles lifted his face heavenward and groaned. *A bridal shop, Lord? Not to sound ungrateful, but You couldn't have made it a tailor shop? And not some place full of women?* Seeing as he had no other choice, he waddled as quickly as he could to the bridal shop and let himself in, sending the copper bell above the door jingling and announcing his presence. Giles took a quick gander and sighed with relief. No women in sight.

From the back of the shop, a lilting voice greeted him from behind the curtain divider, "Welcome to Thimbles and Threads! Please take a seat. I'll be with you in a minute."

Sinking onto the tufted lavender settee, Giles ran his fingers around the brim of his stiff hat and studied the shop that was painted in a soft mint green and French cream trim. The front windows on either side of the door displayed a massive wedding dress in each along with an array of items to draw customers in from the street to view the well-stocked shelves of lace, gloves, veils, and all sorts of wedding paraphernalia that he had no idea existed until now. *Definitely a place for the ladies,* he surmised as he heard the click of heeled shoes on the wood floor and spied a tall, willowy young woman with full lips, fiery curls, and piercing indigo eyes pushing aside a curtain separating the workroom from the shop.

For a moment, Giles forgot why he was sitting in a bridal shop.

ALICE SET the gloves she was mending aside on the shop counter and smiled at the towering, athletic-looking gentleman who was sitting stiffly on her settee, blinking at her with his mouth slightly ajar. She gave him a tentative nod, unsure if he was quite well or if he was merely one of the many fiancés sent on an errand, overwhelmed by all the bobbles of a bridal shop. "Good afternoon, I'm Miss Turner. Can I assist you with something? Are you here to pick up an order for someone?"

"Uh, yes." He rose, gave her a small bow, and instantly returned to the seat, raking his fingers through his thick, wavy coal-black hair and turning his tidy pompadour into a riotous mess. "I'm here for uh. . .well, it's rather hard to explain."

Used to the peculiar responses of males in her shop, Alice simply folded her hands in front of her day gown and studied the striking man in front of her, waiting patiently.

His throat bobbed as he swallowed before giving a cough, as if his words were difficult to release. "I am in need of your assistance. You wouldn't happen to have any ready-made pants in the back, would you? I seem to have had a bit of a mishap."

She glanced at his pant legs, but seeing no tear or rip, she tapped her lip and motioned with her finger for him to rise, but he stayed firmly planted in place on the settee. "I haven't dealt with men's trousers in quite some time, but my father taught me everything he knew and since his, uh, retirement, I have turned his tailor shop into a bridal shop. What exactly needs mending? I don't see anything marring your clothing, Mister. . .?"

"Giles. Just Giles." He cleared his throat, crossed his legs at the knee, and drummed his fingers on his thigh. "I'm not sure how to put this delicately, so I'm just going to say it. I used to be quite active until recent months and now, in my present line of work, I do a lot of sitting, and I haven't had a new suit in quite a while." He laughed, revealing a charming small gap between his front teeth as he ran a hand over his strong jawline. "I should have listened to my sister and ordered a new wardrobe, but it's too late now. Today, the sitting finally caught up with me when I bent down to pick up a baseball for a group of boys and, well, my pants have perished, and that is why I am in your bridal shop and at your mercy, sitting in your presence, which is against what society dictates I should do, while I beg for your assistance."

Understanding made her chest swell with a need to burst into laughter, but as she was a professional woman, she swallowed her amusement and motioned for him to move into one of the two dressing rooms lining the right side of her shop. "Please step behind the curtain and remove your trousers so I can set to work on them." She felt the heat rise in her neck as he slowly rose with an embarrassed tint of his own. Alice whipped her back to him to afford him some privacy as he slipped behind the thick powder-blue curtain.

"Miss Turner, do you have anything for me to wear while you mend?" Mr. Giles asked, his voice muffled by the curtain between them.

She bit her lip, thinking of the small trunk of her parents' things in the attic that she hadn't touched in years. She had vowed she would never open it again, but thinking of the man's predicament, she relented. "I do believe I have some old trousers of my father's that you can borrow, but I can tell you right now that they will not fit your frame. My father was quite stout and short, but they will get the job done while you wait."

He poked his head through the curtains, clutching the fabric beneath his chin. "Anything would be most appreciated, my lady."

At the sight of his tousled hair and helpless tone, she couldn't help but shake her head and laugh to herself. "I will fetch them, sir."

Not stopping to dwell on what she was about to do, she ascended the stairs to the third-floor landing and into the stifling attic, sweat beading her forehead almost at once. Her body gravitated to where she knew the trunk would be. It was covered in a thick layer of dust and grime created by the humidity, so she used her handkerchief to flick open the latch. With a resounding creak, the lid cracked open, the scent of sandalwood flooding her. An unexpected ache formed in her heart at the sight of a perfectly folded, unfinished quilt atop her father's things.

She lifted the quilt out of the trunk and stroked the neat stiches, once again stung with her father's choices. Five years ago, she had been sewing the quilt from scrap materials about the shop as a Christmas gift to him, but when the scandal had broken and destroyed their happiness, she had tucked away her father's things along with the unfinished quilt and had intentionally forgotten about it. Now the torrent of memories the quilt held threatened to overwhelm her. Alice dropped the quilt onto the dusty floor and rummaged through the trunk, found the pants, stuffed the quilt back inside, and slammed the lid, wishing she could just as easily banish her feelings and her heart. Trousers in hand, she darted down the stairs, and standing outside the curtain, cleared her throat to alert the gentleman of her presence. "Mr. Giles?"

"Thank goodness. I was hoping you did not abandon me," he replied through the curtain, a forced laugh following. "And it's just Giles, if you please."

"Of course I didn't abandon you. Now, if you please, the pants, Giles." Trading trousers, she nearly laughed again as she examined the rip, grabbed her basket of scrap materials, and sank onto the settee to mend the seam by hand. *Professional. Be professional.* She was rummaging through the scraps to find some cloth similar in color when she heard the curtain rings scrape against the rod and her customer stepped out in her father's pants. This time, there was no escaping her laughter at the sight of him with his suspenders holding up the ample waistline of the pants and the hem cinched up to his calves, which thankfully were still covered by his navy hosiery, saving them both from further discomfiture.

He whistled through his teeth, his gaze on the large patch in her hand. "Can't you save them?"

She pinned the patch into place. "I'm afraid not, but the patch should be hidden enough under your coat for you to hail a carriage for home without fear of being arrested." She grinned at his reddening cheeks and lowered her gaze, stitching away. "So, tell me what sort of work you did prior to all this sitting?"

He joined her on the settee, watching her work. "I was a tennis instructor at the All England Lawn Tennis Club."

This brought her head up. "What, in London? What an exciting occupation! I've always enjoyed reading about tennis matches and have longed to learn, but—" She lifted his pants. "I'm afraid seamstresses don't make enough for the club fees, much less enough for an instructor. Did you play in the Gentleman's Championship in Wimbledon?"

He grinned. "You've heard of Wimbledon? You really do enjoy the sport. Yes, I've played there the last three years. I placed well, but didn't win, a fact that my father does not fail to remind me."

"What an honor!" She checked her enthusiasm and returned to the pants, making quick work of the remaining stitches. "Here you go, Giles." She handed them to him. "I suggest you buy a new wardrobe as soon as you are able. I'm afraid that if the rest of your pants have this much wear, they won't last long, and you'll be in here again." She grinned. *Though it wouldn't be the worst thing in the world if you were to return.*

CHAPTER TWO

A shimmering sapphire gown and fiery curls drew Giles's gaze to the threshold of the family drawing room, his heart hammering at the sight of her. *What is she doing here?* He swallowed. Despite his mortification at seeing the pretty seamstress who had saved him at his brother's engagement dinner, a thrill traveled through him. Taller than most women, but willowy and graceful, Miss Turner cut an impressive figure in the room of Charleston's socialites.

Clapping his younger brother William on the shoulder and nodding to Meg, he excused himself from the enamored couple and crossed the room, weaving through and around clusters of guests, his gaze never leaving her as she moved toward his brother's bride-to-be.

She began to pass him without seeing him, so he boldly reached out to her only to brush his fingertips on the short satin sleeves of her evening gown. "Miss Turner?"

Her indigo eyes widened and a dimple appeared in her left cheek as she smiled. "Giles? *Just* Giles," she teased. "Whatever are you doing here?"

"I was going to ask you the same. Are you here for. . ." He left off the end of his sentence, fearing it would be rude to assume that she was here only to work when she was dressed as one of the party.

"For taking the bridal party's measurements?" She laughed, shaking her head, dispelling any awkwardness he felt in his lingering question with her brilliant, full smile. "Not at the moment. I'm here as a bridesmaid to one of the brides-to-be. Meg and I have been friends since childhood. Her family's fortune wasn't made until she was nearly sixteen. But as I haven't met you until you visited my shop"—she looked up to him with those bewitching eyes—"I presume you are acquainted with the groom."

"Well, I wasn't his friend by choice, but over the years, we have come to endure one another's company at home and the workplace."

"Ah." She smiled and nodded. "You are the brother of the groom. A fact I should have pieced together, given you two look so much alike."

"Do you have any siblings of your own who help you at the shop?" Giles asked, eager to learn more about her. While he had been at her mercy in the shop, he had refrained from much small talk other than tennis, uncomfortable with his vulnerable appearance.

"I'm afraid that I was the first and last child, as my mother died in childbirth. Though my father was only five and twenty at the time, he never remarried, so I am the sole owner of the shop."

"I'm surprised your father retired so early in life. One would think a tailor of his age would only now be reaching the height of his popularity."

"It was an unexpected choice." She dipped her head, fiddling with the trim on her matching fan. He began to wonder what she wasn't revealing about her father, but before he could inquire further, she nodded to the corner of the room where Meg and William stood arm in arm. "If you'll excuse me, the bride is motioning for me."

He watched her retreating back, intrigued with the woman. He would have to arrange to sit next to her at dinner, even if it meant crossing his sister by switching Miss Turner's place with Miss Castle's. He motioned the butler over and whispered his instructions.

"But Miss Constance specifically—"

He clapped the butler on the shoulder. "I'll take care of my sister. Any wrath I ensue is worth it to sit next to such a captivating dinner partner."

How did he manage to find out bits of my life so easily? Alice shook her head to free herself from the fog of his presence. Giles could never be anything more than a customer, and she would not tell him her life's story. But it was rather pleasant to find the handsome gentleman from her shop, whom she had found herself thinking of throughout her week, at the party she had been dreading. She flicked open her silk fan, with its dainty floral-and-gold design catching in the candlelight, and gave a cursory glance over her shoulder. She smothered a smile when she caught Giles staring at her yet. *Stop thinking of his fine eyes and focus.*

Surveying the room for potential customers, she sauntered past a group of mothers on her way to Meg, showing off her stylish dress fashioned freshly from the *Harper's Bazaar* delivered only two days ago. In anticipation of tonight's group of potential clients, she had her seamstress help her finish it last night to capture the attention of all future brides.

Alice pretended not to hear the other women's whispers behind their silk fans as she took a seat on the settee next to the mother of the bride. Mrs. Martin, who gave Alice's hand a friendly pat, returned to her conversation with the other young ladies of marriageable age, speaking, of course, of Meg's wedding. At a break in the conversation, one of the girls commented on the delightful design of Alice's gown. Not wanting to boast of her own work, Alice graciously dipped her head in thanks as Meg and Constance joined them.

"It's Alice's latest piece. Isn't it a wonder what she can create? I'm thrilled that both Constance and I will be wearing an Alice Turner original gown for our double wedding along with our bridesmaids," Meg announced. Her unabashed admiration caused all the ladies to turn their attention toward Alice.

"I've been wanting to ask if you studied in France?" Miss Hyacinth asked, her gaze scrutinizing every tuck and fold of Alice's handiwork.

"Unfortunately, no. However, my father worked in Paris until he married and moved here to open his own shop, so my styles are French influenced."

At this, Miss Hyacinth's stiff gaze softened to that of a smirk. "Ah, now I know where I've heard the name of Turner. Wasn't your shop originally Turner's Fine Tailor previous to—what's the name again?"

"Thimbles and Threads Bridal Shop," Alice answered, her cheeks burning.

"That's quite the mouthful, but I can't quite place the reason why it changed over to you." She tapped her fan to her chin, lifting her gaze to the ceiling as if trying to recall the scandal that had almost ruined Alice.

Meg placed her arm around Alice's waist in a gentle reminder to remain calm. "I'm sorry to speak out of turn, and I know we weren't really planning on dancing, but William needs far more practice than a week can give." She turned to Constance. "Since your Eustace is out of town until the wedding, would you mind playing the piano so we can practice the quadrille? No one is quite as accomplished as you."

Constance gave her a pretty smile. "You

are too kind to me. I wish Eustace were here, but since he is not, I will sacrifice any chance at dancing this evening and play for you."

Alice sent Meg a small smile, thanking her for her protection. Meg had been like a sister to her since childhood, and even though wealth created a barrier between most people, Alice knew it would never separate them. Hearing the men's voices, she turned her gaze to the double doors to find Hyacinth smiling brilliantly on the arm of Giles as they glided into place to form the sides of the quadrille. Meg smiled back at Alice, took the head position with her fiancé, and nodded to Constance to begin.

Alice clasped her hands behind her back and watched the dancers as they moved in nearly perfect time with the lively music until William lost count of the steps and ran into the back of Miss Hyacinth. But Meg just laughed away the mishap and sent him encouraging smiles throughout the complicated dance. Seeing her friend's adoration for William, Alice felt the hardness of time soften a bit. If Meg could find such joy after going from suitor to suitor in search of a man with character, maybe there was hope for Alice. She supposed that deep down, there was a part of her that longed for the warm embrace of a husband, someone to protect her from the harshness of life. . .or at least, be there to share life's burdens with one another. She sighed. She had long since surrendered that dream, and it would be for the best that she not take it up again.

With the quadrille in its final steps, Alice turned away, intent on finding a quiet corner for a moment of peace to gather her thoughts before sharing dinner with a stranger for a partner. She wasn't used to socializing with the people whom she was trying to secure as her clients, and it was exhausting to be so aware at all moments of potentially saying the wrong thing. When she measured ladies or hemmed gowns, she could remain mostly silent, intent on her work, but here, at a party she was expected to— She jumped at the hand at her elbow.

"May I have the honor of this next dance? Meg has requested a waltz." Giles bowed to her, offering her his hand even as she spied Miss Hyacinth in the corner glaring at her. Not quite sure how to refuse without insulting a client's brother, she nodded, placing her hand in his massive one, feeling petite for the first time in her life.

Constance jammed her fingers on the keys, sounding an introductory chord, garnering the attention of all as she stood and announced, "We don't want our impromptu dancing to ruin the chef's menu."

Meg and William moaned, protesting in unison, "Just one more dance!"

Constance barely disguised the scowl forming over her brow and with a forced smile, returned to her seat. "As you wish it, but this is the *last* dance before dinner, my dear brother and future sister."

Alice could have laughed at how threatened Constance seemed to be. Did she honestly think her brother could be interested in pursuing a seamstress? He was only being kind as he had in her shop when he told her about the tennis championships. But as Giles began to whirl her about the room in a looping, dipping waltz, she felt herself grow a bit lightheaded, and she had to admit to herself that she was quite enjoying the athletic feel of her handsome partner's thick arms. *You will not be caught up in the romance of one evening and one dance,* she scolded herself. But, for that one moment, nothing else existed.

She could hardly recall the music ending when Giles bowed to her and the couples breathlessly applauded Constance as the butler appeared in the doorway. She noticed the butler's gaze fall directly on her partner and give him the smallest nod, motioning the underbutlers to open the double doors and announcing dinner.

Giles bowed to her, obviously not seeing Miss Hyacinth expectantly craning her neck in their direction. "Shall I escort you to your seat?"

"O-of course," she stammered under the glares of Miss Hyacinth and Miss Constance. The moment her hand was tucked in the crook of his arm, she thought for certain Miss Hyacinth would faint. Miss Constance rustled over to them so quickly, Alice thought her bustle was in danger of flying off.

"Giles, don't you think you should escort your dinner partner?" Miss Constance nodded to Miss Hyacinth in the corner, who was desperately fanning her cheeks.

"Miss Turner *is* my dinner partner." Giles gave her a wide-eyed stare. "I made certain to check the table arrangement as you told me to, and that's what the dinner cards decreed."

"What?" She gave Alice a smile that could only be described as a grimace. "I'm so sorry, Miss Turner, but there has been some mistake and I must insist—"

"No need to apologize." Giles steered Alice toward the dining room with a smile and nod to Miss Hyacinth as an elderly gentleman hefted himself out of the armchair by the dormant fireplace and made his way toward Giles's rejected partner. "I shall see to our dear Miss Turner. I know our great-uncle will take great care of Miss Hyacinth as her escort."

Alice found herself standing in front of the elaborate dinner table set with the family's finest china with a short, wide arrangement of white lilies, gardenias, and roses framed by a silver candelabra on either side. She swallowed as Giles held the back of her mahogany chair and every eye turned to them once again. She sank onto the cushioned seat and ran her fingers around the length of her ivory napkin, draping it over her sapphire skirts. She wasn't prepared to chat with a groomsman, much less Giles! *Why didn't Meg warn me?*

"So, you mentioned you longed to learn tennis." Giles went on as if all were normal.

"Y-yes," she stuttered as a gold-rimmed china bowl of turtle soup was placed in front of her.

"Well, my home is only about three miles or so from your shop, and I happen to have a tennis court set up on my lawn." He lifted his soup spoon after his sister, the hostess and second bride-to-be, had taken her first sip.

"Oh, so you *still* play?"

He chuckled and broke off a piece of his sweet-potato roll. "That hard to tell, huh? I guess when one splits his pants from sitting too much it doesn't lead you to assume that said pants-splitter still attempts to exercise."

She diverted her attention to taking a sip of her lukewarm thick soup, unused to teasing and not knowing how to respond. "When did you return to Charleston?"

"After I lost a tournament in the spring. With my father's approaching retirement, I knew it was time to quit my pursuit and join the family business."

Her heart clenched. She knew what it was like to have to surrender to the responsibilities of life. She had once dreamed of becoming a wife and mother, but life had other plans for her. "I'm sorry."

He shrugged as if it had not been a sacrifice. "I loved playing and teaching, but banking also holds my interest. And what of you? How did you come to fancy the sport?"

"As children, Meg and I enjoyed playing badminton together in the park, but when she became a lady, her mother encouraged her to give up the sport." She wiped her mouth with her napkin. "But, as I can't afford to join a club, I watch from a distance or read about matches whenever I am able."

"Well, how about you and I have a match? I promise to go easy on you."

Alice blinked. *He knows I'm just a seamstress, so surely he isn't insinuating that he actually wishes me to play him. . .?* "I'm afraid you have overestimated my badminton skills, and I have never actually had the chance to play tennis."

"Then I'll give you lessons! It has been rather difficult on me giving up instructing since leaving London, and I think we could help each other out. I can teach, you can learn, and we can play, keeping me in better shape."

Better shape? Is that even possible? Alice could feel her cheeks grow warm from secret admiration. She knew she should decline, but her stomach fluttered at the prospect of learning to play the sport. "I don't know what to say."

"Say yes. I can have a carriage drive you to and from your shop so you won't miss your appointments with your clients, and you'd be helping me out by keeping me from going mad shut up in an office all day every day, shuffling paperwork." He lifted his hand. "Not that I dislike my work, but a fellow needs to have a sport to keep active, else risk developing a banker's paunch."

She pressed her napkin to the corner of her mouth again, considering his proposal. The man really did sound quite miserable, and it would be wonderful to take some time for herself. She hadn't really had much of a break since she started her bridal business. She lifted her gaze to see if anyone had overheard his gallant offer to teach her, but besides the pursed lips of Miss Constance from the opposite end of the table, everyone else was busy speaking with one another. "What should I expect to pay per lesson?"

Leaning forward, he said in a conspiratorial whisper, "Would the pleasure of your company over a glass of lemonade after each match on my family's riverboat be too much to ask?"

She choked on her drink and coughed, holding her hand over her mouth. "A riverboat? You jest."

He shrugged. "It's not as grand as it sounds. It's secondhand and quite old, but it gets the family to and from the plantation to visit others."

Rich people. She nearly rolled her eyes, but the thought of finally learning to play tennis was too tempting to pass up. "I will, on one condition." She nodded toward Constance. "We must keep it a secret. I don't want your sister to catch wind of our lessons and think there is anything more to them than getting us both outside for a few hours. Just the hint of gossip could ruin my business and every hope I have of breaking into the elite set of society."

"Of course. And you know we won't ever really be alone. The servants will be there, but I'll make sure they won't say a word."

She extended her hand to him. "Very well, sir. You have yourself a deal. When do we start?"

"My sister makes her morning calls every Monday. So how does that sound?" He waited for her answer as the footman removed their soup dishes.

"I say it will give me just the right amount of time to whip up a tennis gown."

CHAPTER THREE

Alice stepped down from the carriage, gripping the tennis racket that Giles had sent to her shop that morning with a friendly note reminding her of their appointment. She held on to the brim of her hat as she craned her neck back to take in the two-story plantation. With its veranda that wrapped around both floors and massive white columns, it was quite impressive. She swallowed. *Could a man who comes from all this wealth really wish to spend time with me?* Making her way down the gravel path around the big house of the plantation and to the back lawn to where Giles had said to meet him, she couldn't help but take a quick glance up to the long windows to see if she could spy his family inside.

Her breath caught at the wide lawn that stretched from the house to the winding Ashley River, where a riverboat was docked beside the cypress trees that lined the river. And even from that distance, she could tell it was far grander than the small, second-hand paddleboat Giles had described. This steamer could easily carry a hundred passengers, if not more.

She pulled at her lace-trimmed collar. It was going to be another blazing day. *Thank goodness Giles had the wherewithal to schedule a morning lesson.* As Giles was nowhere to be seen, she sank in the manicured grass beneath an oak cloaked in Spanish moss in sight of the lawn tennis court and arranged the skirts of her tennis costume over her ankles, secretly admiring the gown that she had altered from her simplest walking gown. Having adjusted a few of the intricate tucks, she'd arranged the folds of her skirt in a manner that would allow her limbs a little more room to lunge for tennis balls.

She stroked the navy-and-white striped gown, loving the way her skirt fell and how free she felt without the layers upon layers of constricting clothing. *Well, even if I can't hit the ball over the net, I'll at least look the part.*

Nervous that she had arrived too early and was in danger of running into Giles's family, she checked her small watch pin again, absentmindedly rubbing her finger over the engraved pair of silver lovebirds. She was so deep in possible scenarios explaining Giles's absence that at the touch to her elbow, she jumped and inadvertently whacked the man at her side with her racket. At his cry, she looked up into the hazel eyes of her victim.

"Giles! I mean, Mr. Clayton."

"Quite a backhand you have there, Miss Turner," he chuckled, rubbing his elbow. "I didn't think you'd be this cross with my being five minutes late. I couldn't find my shoes. My valet had decided they were far too dirty and had taken them away last night to clean them without telling me."

Her cheeks reddened. "I'm so sorry. I didn't hear you come up behind me."

"Well, I certainly hope that was the case. Otherwise, it would appear that you don't like me very much." He sent her a wink, stilling the rising guilt in her heart. "Just a good thing you didn't knock me in the head, or else I might never recover." He spun his racket in his right hand's loose grip. "If you are ready, let's get started with the basic strokes."

He demonstrated a forehand grip, which she mimicked easily, so he moved on to the backhand, which she did not copy quite as well.

"You almost had it. Return to the forehand position, bring the racket across your body, and *then* add your second hand to the handle."

She scrunched her mouth and attempted it.

"Perfect. Now, turn your shoulders along with your body in a single, fluid motion, like this." He hammered the ball over the net.

After a few false starts, she managed at least to get the ball over the net, and they moved on to service strokes. She watched closely as he tossed the ball up with one hand and came down on it with his racket at a precise angle, sending the ball bouncing to the correct opposite box.

Alice threw the ball up into the air, swung, and missed, the ball hitting her atop her head. She rubbed the spot, scowling, and tried again and again, to no avail.

He rubbed his hand over his chin. "Hmm, why don't we try to simply volley back and forth to get you used to hitting the ball first, and practice switching your grip from forehand to backhand?"

"That might be for the best. Serving is a lot harder than it looks." She laughed, wiping her forehead with the cuff of her sleeve. *Blast this sun.* She really did not enjoy being so sweaty in front of such a handsome instructor.

He trotted to the other side of the net and took his position. "Okay, I'm going to send the ball your way. Let it bounce once and then hit it back to me." He executed a perfect forehand, sending the ball flying over the net.

She waited for the bounce and tried to

swing, but the pesky ball was coming straight toward her. With a squeal, she held the racket up to block her face. "I thought you were going to go easy on me," she protested, feeling her face redden but not from the heat of the sun.

He chuckled. "I was. You forgot to move to the side of the ball and were taking it straight on." He moved his stance from side to side in a quick stride-hop motion that had her scratching her head.

"Easy enough," she called in a false bravado and took her stance again, ready this time.

The ball came over the net and bounced once. She moved to the side and whipped her racket, expecting a *whack* and was met with a *whoosh.* She had missed. "Again!"

NOT WANTING her to become discouraged, Giles waved the tennis ball over his head, staying her swing before she could miss and send another ball flying backward into the Ashley River or smacking into the net. It was a miracle she hadn't lobbed a ball through one of the long windows of the house. "You've done wonderfully for your first lesson, but let's say we call it a day?"

"Oh, I thought we'd have an actual match?"

"I'm glad you still want to play after, uh —" He stopped short of saying "a disastrous lesson" and instead, grinned and said, "An intense first lesson, but we may be a lesson or two away from playing a set. Shall we take our refreshment now?" He offered her his arm, thankful that he hadn't perspired much. "I'm pretty sure it is lawn tennis rules that the instructor must give his student lemonade or risk dishonor."

She checked her watch again and appeared to be weighing his offer before she nodded and dropped the watch pin against her bodice. "I did promise you one glass, but then I must hurry back to the shop to change and meet with my new clients. I have a bride who is getting married in three days, and this is her final fitting. I want her to be as calm as possible, and my being late would not only upset her but also potentially lose me a future client in her sister."

"But why limit yourself to wedding dresses"—he gestured at her creative tennis ensemble, which he knew his sister would buy in an instant—"when you are obviously gifted in all styles?"

"Because I want to be known for my wedding dresses someday and not just be that seamstress who makes stylish dresses. I want the Turner name to stand for something beautiful, something pure, and not. . ." She drifted off as they stepped onto the plank of the riverboat. He led her up a flight of stairs to a deck with a wide promenade overlooking the water with a decorative railing painted in a pretty soft white. Her smile widened at a pair of wicker chairs on the deck, facing the river, with a glass pitcher of lemonade and two cups on a small table. "Well, this is lovely."

He gestured for her to take a seat. "Thank you. We could use the main cabin where my family usually dines while on the river, but I figured we didn't want to be inside when we had the chance to enjoy a bit of a breeze from the river." Giles lifted a pitcher and poured them each a tall glass of iced lemonade. He handed one to her, fascinated with learning more about her and loving the sprinkle of freckles appearing on her nose after a morning in the sunshine.

"Returning to what you were saying, I think I understand. I wanted my name to stand for more than just a family-owned bank, but life had other plans." He ran his finger over the rim of his glass. "I know that one day tennis won't be seen just as a pastime, but it amazes me how many people consider my time in London playing as merely the hobby of a young man who wasn't ready to accept life's responsibilities. It's different over there. If people here knew how much training it takes to play in Wimbledon. . .they wouldn't be so condescending." He laughed and ran his fingers through his hair. "I apologize for being so morose. I had rather a ridiculous encounter at the office as I was leaving to come for our lesson, and it rubbed me the wrong way."

"No need to apologize." She reached out and brushed her fingertips over his knuckles, but before he could even look up at her, she pulled her hand away and dipped her head as if suddenly aware of her impropriety. "I know what it's like not to be taken seriously. When my father left and I took over, the other shops on King Street thought I'd be closing within a month. They considered me a little girl playing at being a tailor." She lifted her glass. "And yet, I'm still here and my shop is still running, so they've begun to give me more respect as the years go by and as I get older. I hope for you that it is only a matter of time as well."

"Thank you." He smiled softly, dazed at her opening up to him. "Well, I am thankful that one of us is respected in our profession." And he meant every word. The more glimpses he got into this young lady's life, the more he admired her for persevering.

Shifting in her seat, seeming uncomfortable with the turn the conversation had taken, she downed her lemonade in three gulps and set it aside, rising. "I really must be going. I didn't realize how late the hour had become. I don't want to risk running into your family and raising an alarm when it is not warranted. Thank you for the refreshment."

He swallowed back his grin at her unladylike, albeit endearing, action as he rose to follow her to the carriage, not willing to part from her quite yet. "May I drive you home? I took the liberty of asking the stable boy beforehand to ready the buggy instead of the carriage."

"Well, as it is *your* buggy that is bringing me back, I can't rightly say no." She sent him a wry smile, but he could tell from her tone that she was pleased at his request—at least, he hoped that is what he heard in her voice. "But we best make haste. I need to take care of Cat prior to my next appointment." She gathered her beaded reticule and racket, fairly racing down the steps and descending the plank to the dock.

"Cat? You mean, you have a cat, or is that your pet's name?" he asked as he strode down the path after her.

"Cat is his name." She glanced over her shoulder at him as if it were the most natural name in the world.

He rubbed his hand over his mouth,

fearing laughter would not endear him to her. Giles waved off the groomsman and assisted Alice into the buggy himself. After taking up the reins and giving them a little snap, he cleared his throat. "So, Cat. Why did you settle upon that name?"

She lifted her hand, shielding her eyes from the sun. "I didn't want to get too attached to him."

"He's a new pet to you?"

"I've had him for four years." She smiled as if quite aware of how confusing her words were. "But that doesn't mean he's getting another name. I don't trust he will stay."

He laughed as he turned the horse onto the road. "I'd say he's staying, but that's just my humble opinion."

The drive to King Street passed so quickly, Giles considered "accidentally" taking her around the block again, but knowing she had a client, he saw her to her shop door. Before she stepped inside, he grasped her by the elbow, turning her to him. "May I call on you?" He watched her lips twist with what appeared to be trepidation, and he began to think his chances were slim if not next to none.

“I’m going to be quite busy for the next month with all the summer weddings, and I’m already stretching my schedule by taking two hours every Monday to practice tennis with you, but once this month is over, and if you still feel the same, maybe you could ask me again?” She glanced up at him, an enchanting glint in her indigo eyes.

Giles lifted a finger. “One month?”

“One month.”

He grinned and extended his hand. “It’s a deal.”

CHAPTER FOUR

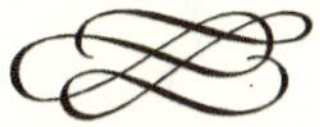

In the week following their first lesson, Alice half expected Giles to cancel. After all, she was only a seamstress, and he was a partner at a successful bank, so why was he interested in spending time with her? But true to his word, his carriage showed up at the exact time every week and continued to show up in the weeks following, gently reminding Alice of her promise to step out with him, cracking the wall in her heart with every sweet smile he sent her way. And as she grew more capable with a racket, she found herself enjoying his companionship even more.

It was nice to have someone to talk to besides Meg. With her wedding and her sister's debut coming up, Meg was often too busy to even have a cup of tea, leaving Alice with no one to converse with but Giles. To her surprise, he had proven himself to be a good listener as she talked about lace and ruffles and unhappy clients. And in turn, Giles confided in her about his time in London and of his disappointment over losing his last tournament, along with his struggles with becoming a banker and accepting the responsibilities that were laid upon him. Over their weekly pitcher of lemonade after their lesson, they formed a friendship that was sweet and treasured by both. Now with only a few days in the agreed-upon month until Giles asked her to dinner again, Alice was surprised to find that she was going to release all her inhibitions and accept. Their lessons had become the highlight of her week, and she ached to see him in the days between.

She was thankful that today, Meg's wedding day, she would spend the entire morning and afternoon with him and not just a few stolen minutes after a tennis lesson. When the clock on the mantel chimed eight times, she finished buttoning the back of her powder-blue bridesmaid gown and, yelling a good morning and goodbye to Cat, she gripped her satchel of sewing supplies and darted down the sidewalk toward Meg's home, breathing heavily as she rounded the corner and let herself in through the side gate. Taking the servant's entrance that was always open, Alice raced up the busy staircase to Meg's room on the second floor. Slipping off the light shawl she wore to keep the dust of the streets at bay, she stepped into the bustling room as the two brides and Miss Hyacinth, the other bridesmaid, made last-minute touches to their ensembles.

"Thank goodness you are here." Mrs. Martin grasped her arm and pulled her to Meg's side. "My daughter has been so nervous, she's been overeating, and well, we burst three of the buttons on her gown before we managed to tighten her corset and close the back."

"I'm so sorry. I thought we were helping her dress at half past eight."

"I wanted to start early because I knew something was going to go wrong." Meg's voice cracked as she waved her hands, fanning her face to keep her tears at bay. "People have been inserting their opinions all week regarding my choice of timing the first dance *after* our breakfast feast, the actual dance I've chosen, and even going so far as to question *why* we are dancing at all. And to top it all off, nearly every other woman I've encountered this week has inquired why I have broken from tradition and didn't ask my sister to be my bridesmaid." She hiccupped, her tears beyond control. "Does no one understand that it is *my* wedding day, and I'm doing what makes me happy? And now my dress won't be perfect."

Alice gently rubbed Meg's shoulder and pulled her into a hug. "Never you mind what people say. And as for your dress, it is a simple fix." She removed her sewing kit from her satchel, bent behind her friend, and proceeded to sew the silk-covered buttons back into place. "There. No harm done."

"Except that now I can't breathe from the tightness of my corset strings!" Meg pressed a hand to her waist. "Oh, why did I eat that last roll at breakfast?"

"Because sometimes even the most disciplined of us can't resist cinnamon rolls dripping in vanilla icing, but on occasions when one has to fit into a dress, it is best if you refrain from indulging your every craving day in and day out." Constance patted her perfectly coiled and pinned raven locks as she slowly spun in front of the looking glass, admiring her wedding gown. "I hope Eustace recognizes the great pains I have taken to embody the pet name he has given me."

"Oh?" Meg asked, "And what would that be?" She twisted her mouth toward Alice and whispered, "Miss Constantly Prissy, perhaps?"

Alice snorted into her hands, choking on her suppressed laughter.

"Angel, of course." Constance rolled her eyes.

Alice stiffened. Angel had been *her* Eustace's pet name for her. What were the odds that Constance was marrying another man named Eustace who used that pet name with his fiancée? *Don't be paranoid. It is a common enough term of endearment. You should be over this nonsense of even caring,* she chided herself. She checked her hair for any strands out of place as the clock chimed the ninth hour. "One more hour, Meg," Alice sang out, grasping her friend's hands and spinning her about the room.

"You'll wrinkle her!" Miss Hyacinth protested, but was ignored amid the giggling.

"I've asked Giles to act as your escort for the wedding. I hope you don't mind?" Meg's eyes sparkled as if she already knew long ago that Alice was secretly attracted to Giles. She leaned in and whispered, "Between you and me, even though Giles is standing with my William, I was hard pressed to convince Constance that he should be your escort and not Miss Hyacinth's knight in shining armor, because apparently Constance believes that they are *destined* to wed."

Even though Alice was miffed at the heat crawling up her neck, she could not bring herself to protest, which she was certain betrayed her feelings upon the matter as she normally would've objected to any such arrangement. She tilted her head, pursed her lips, and lifted her brows at Meg. *Of course she knows I like Giles.* In the few moments she and Meg had spent together all month, all Alice had been able to talk about was her diverting tennis lessons with said groomsman. "I suppose you want me to say thank you?"

Meg kissed her on the cheek. "Yes, but not until you are safely engaged to your Giles."

"Meg!" She gasped, pulling her away from the others. "He is *not* my Giles, and you best not let anyone hear you saying such things."

Meg giggled. "I overheard him speaking to *my* William in the study, and I can tell you that he is quite smitten with you."

Alice dared not allow her heart believe

those words and recounted to herself again the reasons why she and Giles could never be anything other than friends. *I am a seamstress. He is a successful banker, rapidly climbing society's rungs and getting even further out of my reach, which is most likely the reason why he is so comfortable around me. I'm not even on his mind as a potential bride.* She dropped her hands. "If anyone should think I am a flirt, my business will suffer."

Meg's brows raised. "Oh, and speaking of your business, I also wanted to let you know that your gowns are a colossal success. I have overheard Constance comment on the workmanship to multiple guests throughout the week."

"High praise indeed," she whispered to Meg, giggling as they pulled on their white kid gloves.

"The carriages are here! Girls, gather around for your instructions." Meg's mother clapped her hands together, gathering everyone to her with the flutter of her silk fan above her head. With her slim figure, Mrs. Martin looked like she could be one of the girls herself if not for streaks of dove gray appearing in her blond curls. "The brides will be escorted to the church by the parents. Miss Castle, you will be escorted by Eustace's groomsman, and, of course, that leaves Miss Turner to Mr. Clayton's care. Now, as this is a double wedding, there will be a large number in attendance, so Miss Turner and Miss Castle, you two will need to attend Meg and Constance unceasingly to keep guests from lingering too long at their tables. The brides must be allowed to eat. Go to your escort downstairs and stay with them for the duration of the wedding and reception *beside* your bride. Your groomsman will act as your partner as well as your butler so that you don't leave your bride unless it is for attending their errand. Now, enough talk." She waved her fan again. "We have a wedding to attend!"

The girls tittered among themselves, hiding their giggles behind their silk fans.

Alice gave Meg's fingers a squeeze and whispered, "You are a vision."

Meg dipped her head. "I fear all these ruffles and laces are the true beauty."

Alice adjusted the bow at Meg's hip. "I

wasn't referring to the gown. A bride's radiance brings life to my gowns, not the other way around, my friend."

Meg gave her a peck on the cheek. "This morning, I wed my Prince Charming and one day soon, I hope you will wed yours as well. Give Giles a chance and say yes to dinner."

Only a few weeks ago, Alice would've declared that she would never meet a man who would cause her to dream again, but that was before Giles appeared in her shop. "Maybe I already decided I will," she admitted softly. *Even if I can never call him mine.*

"Alice Turner!" Meg giggled. "Will miracles never cease? You had best go find Mr. Giles Clayton and get better acquainted before you change your mind. If he is *not* your Prince Charming, then at least be friends, for he is my brother now. . . Well, in an hour he will be."

Alice stepped into the main foyer to find Giles waiting beyond the front threshold on the top step, his thumbs looped in the pockets of his silk waistcoat as he tilted his black top hat to block the morning light.

"Good morning, *Mr. Clayton.*" Alice smiled up at him, enjoying the fact that he was one of the few men she had encountered who were tall enough for her to look up to.

His brows rose at her formality. "I thought we were past that, *Miss Turner.*" He sent her a wink.

She inclined her head toward the carriage, whispering, "Except when we might be overheard by your sister or any guest who will report to your sister. You know as well as I do that it would cause an unnecessary stir." She placed her hand in the crook of his arm for him to lead her out to the carriage where Miss Hyacinth and her escort were already settling inside.

Alice and Giles took their seats opposite the couple, and Alice arranged her skirts about her so they wouldn't crumple. She glanced up to find Miss Hyacinth's dark-brown eyes piercing into her, shifting to Giles and alighting with a smile.

"Giles." She drew his name out, brazenly

using his Christian name. "I had hoped to spend some more time with you after your call this week."

Alice's heart hammered in her chest and she endeavored not to glance at Giles. *He called on her? After all his bravado of asking me out, he was merely teasing.* She felt her throat close with suppressed disappointment. She knew she shouldn't be surprised, but Giles had seemed so sincere in his attentions to her.

"Well, uh. . ." He appeared to be glancing at Alice, but as she refused to look at him, she couldn't be certain. "I enjoyed our discussion as well, but I was sorry that your father had to cancel our appointment after my arrival. Your father had some investment opportunities he wished to discuss, so I might try to catch him at the reception if there's a moment."

Miss Hyacinth gave a lilting laugh, pressing her hand to her ruffled chest. "Just like Papa. Always working." She leaned forward, adding, "It reveals a depth of character that is quite attractive to a woman."

Alice bit back a gasp at the girl's scandalous flirting. She averted her gaze to the window. Flirting was a luxury of the wealthy. If she dared say such a thing, she would be labeled as a—well, she would never flirt.

"I believe we are in the presence of another hard worker. Miss Turner, I heard you designed the brides' and maids' gowns, did you not?" Giles turned to her, but Alice knew full well he was aware that she had.

She dared not meet his gaze, not with Miss Hyacinth there, but where else was she to look, her lap again? She swallowed and lifted her head. "Yes. Do you like them?"

His gaze flowed over her light-blue gown with its cream trimmings of lace and ribbon, not in a way that would make her cringe, but rather as someone regarding a piece of art with admiration and respect. "I cannot imagine how you come up with such intricate designs."

Miss Hyacinth's lips pursed and she cleared her throat. "I must admit that I wished to have the gowns sent from Paris, but apparently Miss Turner has sunk her hooks into the family and is riding on their coattails to success."

Alice whipped her head to Miss Hyacinth, no longer caring if she was a potential client or not. "I've worked for *everything* I own. It was kind of Meg's family to use me as their seamstress, yes, but I earned the right to garner their interest on my own merit."

Miss Hyacinth gasped and beat her fan, causing a windstorm as she turned to the escort she had been ignoring for the entirety of the trip to Clayton Plantation. Miss Hyacinth made no effort to conceal her haste in exiting the carriage when it rolled to a halt.

Alice, a bit breathless from her altercation, was thankful Giles did not say anything further on the subject and accepted his assistance stepping down from the carriage and up the stairs to the main level of the plantation where the transformed ballroom awaited them. They took their place behind Miss Hyacinth and her escort, waiting for the music and procession to begin. Holding her shoulders back, she tried not to think of all in attendance turning to her before resting their gazes on the brides. *I'm essentially a decoration, a background for the brides, and nothing more. There is no reason to be nervous. I can do this.* She gritted her teeth as the underbutlers drew open the double doors, her pulse quickening at the sight of the crowded plantation ballroom. *At least I can take comfort in the beauty of my gowns and the manliness of my groom—groomsman!* Her palms grew sweaty from her ridiculous thoughts.

When Miss Hyacinth reached the middle of the aisle, Alice began her promenade, smiling and discreetly nodding to anyone she recognized. When she caught sight of Constance's groom for the first time, she stumbled. Giles gripped her arm, righting her at once and keeping his smile firmly in place as she felt heat flood her cheeks. *How can this be?* Giles's sister was marrying a man by the name of Eustace Merrick. . .*not* Eustace Burke, but there was no doubt that her former fiancé stood at the end of the aisle. Her stumble had drawn his attention, and their eyes locked. The groom paled and averted his gaze before anyone could notice what had transpired between them.

He must have changed his name, but does Constance know? She wondered if she should warn Giles's sister, but she wasn't sure if her warning at the altar would come out of a place of malice or kindness, so she remained silent and watched the man she once loved pledge his troth to another.

CHAPTER FIVE

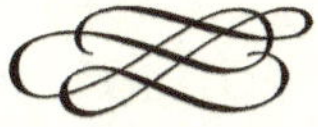

Alice was uncharacteristically mute as Giles escorted her to their place at the breakfast feast, only returning his questions with stilted replies. He glanced up in the direction where her eyes kept drifting. *Merrick. She knows him, but from where?* He had mentioned Eustace's surname at least a dozen times in her presence, and yet she had not given any reaction. Something was not right. When the minister spoke Eustace's name, he had watched her face turn ashen, and he feared she would topple over before the ceremony ended. Holding the back of her chair, Giles caught sight of her trembling hands. "Miss Turner, are you quite well?"

She shook her head as if awakening from a daze. "Water, please."

Giles waved one of the underbutlers over and motioned to her glass. "Water and a couple of dinner rolls if you please."

The young man appeared distressed at the prospect of breaking tradition, but with one glare from Giles, he did as he was told. Giles took his seat beside Alice, and when she had downed her glass of water and discreetly devoured her dinner rolls, he whispered, "Feel any better?"

She nodded. "Thank you. I was in such a rush this morning that I didn't even have time for a bite." She pressed a hand to her corset. "I was afraid my stomach's dissatisfaction was audible in the ceremony."

He wished he could believe that was the only reason for her stricken facial expressions during the ceremony. "I saw you looking at Merrick as if you know him. But in all the times I've ever mentioned him, you never once said you recognized his name."

"I didn't recall the name until I saw his face," she answered, her finger rubbing the gold edge of her china plate as she craned her neck toward the head of the table. "I really should see if Meg needs me."

"Fainting will not help Meg. Besides, if she needs anything, she can beckon you for further assistance." Giles hated to press her, but concern for his sister urged him forward. He cleared his throat. "So, were you well acquainted with Mr. Merrick?"

She shrugged. "A long time ago, but I haven't seen him in years and years." She gave him a smile as if begging to be released from his questioning. "The cake is a masterpiece. Have you seen it?" She gestured to the corner of the room where a massive, four-tiered cake was displayed on its own linen-covered table.

He pretended to admire it, but his mind raced as she continued to point out the decor of the room in an attempt to distract him from Merrick. In his heart, he knew that she must be very well acquainted with the groom, else she would not have had such an adverse reaction to his sister's now husband. His gaze rested on Constance's beaming face as she leaned on Eustace's arm while the first course was brought out.

He had inquired about Mr. Eustace Merrick's character when his sister had first introduced him as a suitor in the spring. However, there wasn't much known about Merrick besides the fact that he was a wealthy owner of a highly successful tailor shop, who claimed that his grandparents were from Scotland. Giles could not locate anyone who knew Merrick more than five years ago, but Merrick had claimed the reason was because he was studying in Paris. Giles was beginning to think that Merrick's success, which seemed to have grown overnight, lent him more credit than Father probably should have given him. Having had no negative responses from their inquiries, they assumed that Eustace told the truth, and Father allowed him to court Constance. Father would never prevent a man who worked himself up from poverty to wealth from proposing to Constance. After all, Father's paternal grandfather had worked himself up from nothing.

But there was something more to this fellow that Alice was not telling him, and his pulse quickened at the thought that his sister had married a stranger.

ALICE FLED THE BREAKFAST ROOM, desperate for a breath of fresh air. Descending the stairs as quickly as her silk slippers would allow, she made her way down the side path and sank down into the curve of a giant oak tree's low branch that rested on the ground. Leaning against the soft bark, Alice sighed. She had done it. She had survived her former fiancé's wedding. On a day that should have been about her best friend, she hated to be distracted with *him*. . .if only Meg hadn't been abroad those two years that Eustace had worked with Father, she might have recognized him. Alice brushed her curls from her face and straightened her shoulders. She had to get control of herself before Meg saw through her facade to her aching heart. It was too late to warn Constance anyway, so she would let the secret lie. Why would she *want* to tell anyone that he was once her own? If word ever—

At the growing laughter and the clink of glasses, Alice twisted around to find the guests had meandered out onto the veranda, chatting as they most likely waited for the ballroom to finish being cleared from the ceremony in preparation for the wedding dance. Alice may have survived the wedding, but she couldn't face Eustace. Not now. She needed a few more moments to compose her thoughts. Continuing down the dirt path that wound through the giant oak trees and was lined with azaleas sprinkled with magenta blossoms, she followed it to where she knew she would find the Ashley River. The path led her to a steep drop to the river and she was faced with a choice, take a right toward the riverboat, where the servants were preparing it to take the two couples downriver, or take a left toward the swamp path that curled around the river by the old rice fields that were no longer in use. She knew she was neglecting her duties as a bridesmaid, but she also knew Meg would understand if she needed to take a quarter of an hour to herself. Alice picked up her pace when she heard footsteps behind her.

"Alice? Is it you?" His deep voice ripped her from the present to the brutal past.

Slowly, hesitantly, Alice turned around to find *him*. She had not allowed herself to study him during the wedding, but she could see that Eustace was unaltered, with his youthful glow still about him. His jaunty smile, and even his wavy light-brown hair held the same brilliance. She had thought that after all this time, her memories had been corrupted and she had glorified his true beauty, but now. . . She could see that he was far more handsome than she had remembered. She flicked open her fan, gently cooling her cheeks, and hoped that she appeared the picture of imperturbable tranquility. "Hello, Mr. *Burke*."

His face darkened. "It's Merrick now, as you've very well heard." He joined her under the shade of the tree without waiting to be invited. "What are you doing here, Alice?"

His impertinent question raised her hackles. How dare he address her by her

Christian name? She glanced over her shoulder, waiting for another guest to appear and save her from conversing with him.

"I go without seeing you for five years, and on the morning of my wedding you magically appear as a *bridesmaid*." He fairly spat the words. "Are you attempting to ruin me, since your father didn't finish the job?"

Her jaw dropped, and the temper she had tried so hard to control threatened to overtake her. She drew a deep breath to slow her racing heart, knowing that if her anger grew too far out of control, she would divulge her true emotions. She would not give him the satisfaction of seeing how much he had hurt her. Even though her motives weren't pure, she sought to keep her soul at peace as best she could. *Help me, Lord. Fill me with Your peace and guard my heart and my mind. You and I both know that I would rather slap him than turn the other cheek.* She eased her fist to lie flat on her skirts as her thundering pulse slowed. "No, Mr. Burke—I mean, Mr. *Merrick*. I am not attempting to ruin you. If you had any memory of our time together, you would recall that Meg is my dearest friend."

"Oh." He shifted his stance and changed tactics as he gave her that coy smile that had once captivated her. "So, tell me, Alice, how are you? I haven't seen you since. . ." His voice drifted off.

"Since you cowardly left me behind to deal with the shards of my father's business after the scandal broke in the papers?" She couldn't help but stab.

"I see you are still bitter about that. Good." He laughed. "If you weren't, then you were not as much in love with me as I was with you."

You certainly had a strange way of showing your devotion. Not deeming him worthy of a reply, she strode away in the direction of the house.

"Well, aren't you going to ask me about how I am doing?" His long strides brought him beside her.

She inwardly cringed at his self-obsession and began to wonder what she had ever seen in him. She had only been a girl when they had begun courting. . .and a girl when he had jilted her. But that day she had become a woman. She didn't wish to know about his life, and she did not have to wait for him to tell her. Alice picked up her pace, eager to distance herself from him.

She may have made her peace with her lot in life, but she was only now beginning to realize the depth of the hurt that she had shoved aside in order to survive. She stopped short, whirled to him, and forced out the words. "Congratulations on your wedding." She added stiffly, "Constance is quite the beauty."

"Yes, she is a picture. Petite, hair the color of the night, with a porcelain complexion and—" He gave her a rueful grin. "Blessed."

Her cheeks flamed at his poor deportment. He would speak so vulgarly of the woman he was supposed to love with his former fiancée? Did Eustace wish her to be jealous of his lady fair's stature? He knew that Alice's height had been a sore spot. Was he attempting to wound her yet? Well, she would not take the bait. She was stronger now and did not need the opinion of a man to validate her beauty. She knew her fiery hair and freckled nose may not be everyone's ideal of beauty, but she fully embraced them as they reminded her daily of her mother, who she had been told had possessed an ethereal beauty. Eustace had pitiable taste to suggest her looks that had once so enchanted him were wanting. She only wished she had seen this side of him years ago so that she had not wasted another breath pining over a man that the Lord had spared her from marrying. "I'm sure Constance will make you the perfect wife." *You best treat her with respect, else Giles will set you straight, if Constance doesn't first.*

He shrugged. "Don't see how she couldn't. She's a banker's daughter and quite wealthy and is very sweet to me. Imagine me climbing the ranks so far as to marry a—"

"Eustace?" Giles appeared at her elbow, drinks in hand. "What are you doing all the way out here with Alice? The opening quadrille is about to begin, and Constance is inquiring after your presence."

Giles's tone exuded displeasure, causing

her to barely cover her smile. For once, she didn't mind a man coming to her aid. She enjoyed seeing the jealousy light in Eustace's expression at the mention of her name.

"Giles? You know Alice?"

Giles ignored his question. "It appears that you do, so it begs the question as to why she bears such a disquieted expression?" He turned to her, concern etched over his brow. "Did he say something to upset you, Alice?"

"Of course not." Eustace lifted his brows as if daring her to say otherwise. "I knew her father quite well, and he inspired my first suits. And now, after years of learning the craft in Paris, I own the most sought-after men's fine apparel tailor shop in Charleston."

Because my father taught you everything he knows about menswear. She grasped the lemonade and downed it as she felt the strain in her lungs growing. She couldn't release her true thoughts, not in front of Giles.

"Giles, will you take me to Meg? She

must be wondering where I am." She boldly grasped Giles's hand and retreated toward the big house, breathing easier with every step she took away from that horrid man.

Miss Hyacinth met them at the foot of the path, her gaze falling on Alice's hand wrapped around Giles's own. Her pink lips pursed as she glared at Alice. "Giles, I saw you come down here with two drinks and thought I'd follow. Thank you for confirming that our dear seamstress really is what I've been thinking." She turned on her heel.

"Miss Castle, it's not—" He called after her retreating figure. "Miss Castle!"

But Miss Hyacinth ignored him, confirming the future demise of Alice's bridal shop with the social elite if she did not remedy this situation at once.

Alice dropped her hold on his hand, sighing. "I'm sorry. I wasn't thinking. I just had to get away from him."

He grasped her elbow, gently turning her to him. "What did Eustace say to you?"

She regarded him, weariness seeming to press her very bones. "I think it might be for the best if we skip Monday's lesson. It's my busy season after all."

"Alice."

"Trust me." It was too late to warn anyone of Eustace's lie, and if she spoke now. . .would he despise her once he knew the truth about why Eustace left her? She bit her lip and fled to the house before she divulged the secret she had been bearing for far too long.

CHAPTER SIX

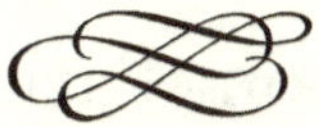

Alice had kept clear of Giles for the rest of the wedding celebration, and when she sent back the carriage on Monday, refusing their lesson, he decided he needed to at least try to convince her to trust him enough to confide in him what she knew of Eustace. Despite his worries, Giles took a small measure of comfort knowing that if she thought Eustace a danger to Constance, she would have spoken up prior to the ceremony. So he was fairly certain Eustace wasn't a criminal, only someone Alice did not particularly like.

The jog to her shop cooled his fevered thoughts. Pausing to wipe away his perspiration, a flash of burgundy caught his attention and he discovered Alice, in a striking gown, working in the display window with her back to him. Giles lingered to watch as she arranged a long veil in the display of what he supposed to be her creations and latest shipment from Paris. She was so engrossed in arranging a fold in the veil in just the right manner that he finally tapped on the windowpane, chuckling as she jumped and nearly dropped the veil.

She turned a scowl to the window, but her agitation evaporated into pleasure when their gaze met before she smoothed her expression. She rolled her eyes and lifted up the veil. "Have you need of this veil?" she called through the wavy glass, motioning him inside and turning to hop out of the display window.

He hurried inside and caught her hands, assisting her descent. "I'll have you know that I didn't even take the time to conjure an excuse to see you." Her hands felt so right in his. *Will she ever allow me the chance to win them?*

"I apologize for sending your carriage

home, but I thought I was clear about canceling today's lesson." Alice dropped her gaze and pulled her hands from his.

"I had hoped you would reconsider, but as you are still opposed, would you be willing to take a short stroll with me instead? I promise I won't ask any prying questions." He stuffed his hands into his tennis trouser pockets and gave her a half smile to assure her of his innocent intentions. "I only thought if you were too busy at the shop for a lesson, you could surely use a short break."

She sighed and seemed to be weighing her options. "I could use a bit of fresh air, I suppose. Let me fetch my chapeau and parasol."

Silently strolling down King Street, Giles wove Alice around the bustling shoppers and errand boys and diverted her toward the park, where the din of the city lessened to a hum and a lone bird chirped in the dogwood and magnolia trees, calling, Giles imagined, for his love. He cleared his throat at the nonsensical thought. Whatever was the matter with him? "Well, I was disappointed you were, uh, detained this morning as I wanted to tell you that I think you are ready to play a tennis match with me."

She halted her promenade down the gravel path, her parasol rolling on her shoulder. "Well, I wouldn't have canceled on you if I had known that!"

"I wanted to surprise you." Giles laughed, feeling the awkwardness of their last interaction melting away in the heat of the day. He had wished to ask her to dinner after their morning lesson, but after her mysterious behavior at the wedding, he feared doing so would scare her away for good. Instead he suggested, "If you find that today wasn't as busy as you thought, why don't you come now? My father will be out on business most of the day, and well, Constance is gone for the week on her wedding trip, so you don't have to worry about running into anyone. It'll just be me and you and the twenty tennis balls that we will have nearby in case you decide to keep sending them flying into the river."

She rolled her eyes, bringing his gaze to

her lovely auburn lashes. "That happened once. If I leave my assistant in charge, you promise we will finally get to play a *full* set and not just hit the ball back and forth without keeping score?"

He grinned. "I'll even let you win a match."

And with that, he found himself fairly trotting to keep up with her as she hurried to her shop, making quick work of changing, placing her assistant in charge, and joining him in the hired carriage.

Giles couldn't help but grin at her eagerness to finally play. *I should've told her she was ready at the wedding and I might have avoided this whole almost skipping practice.* He glanced at her from the corner of his eye as she bounced her racket against her knee.

"I'm glad you came for me." She broke the silence as the carriage wheels crunched the gravel on his driveway. "I can become quite the recluse when I get caught up in my own thoughts." She viewed the scenery, swaying with the turn of the carriage wheels. "And sometimes, I can't even remember how to escape my thoughts on my own, so thank you." She sent him a tentative smile that made his heart ache.

What happened that hurt you? he was tempted to ask, but merely returned her smile and risked giving her hand a quick squeeze. "Anytime."

As the carriage rolled to a stop, her look of consternation vanished as she hopped out of the carriage without waiting for assistance. "Enough of that. It's *finally* time to play!"

ALICE GRUNTED. She would not give him this next point. She bent her knees and readied her racket as Giles positioned himself to toss the ball into the air, calling. "Fifteen love!"

His declaration caused her to stumble and miss her chance to dive for the ball. "What did you just call me?"

His brow creased. "Call you? I was calling the score. Fifteen to love—it's tennis slang for zero."

"Oh." The breath went out of her. "Of

course. I know that from all the matches I've read about." *But it is surprisingly disappointing. Even though it would be ridiculous for him to say he loves me after only knowing me for–* The ball came hurtling over the net directly toward her, but her feet would not move as fast as her brain wanted them to and she tripped, the ball slamming her in the back of her head and sending her sprawling face-first.

"Alice!" Giles vaulted over the net and knelt beside her. "Why didn't you move to the side of the ball like I showed you?"

She twisted her mouth and sputtered out bits of grass. "I was trying to do just that, but you *hurled* the ball at me. And I am pretty certain you said you'd let me win."

"I'm trying to, but I'm afraid you are making it difficult," Giles teased as he helped her to her feet. "Now, are we quite clear on the scoring system?"

Resigned that Giles would win the set, she set her sights on attempting to win the next two. *Whack.* She imagined Eustace's face on the tennis ball as she smacked it with a grunt. Giles's jaw dropped as her passionate strike sent the tennis ball sailing into the river.

By the end of the third set, she was certain she no longer looked as fetching as she had when they first started. Her pretty coiled braid had come loose and tumbled to her waist, but she paid it no mind and brushed away at the perspiration beading on her forehead.

With his racket tucked under his distractingly muscular tan arm, Giles tossed the ball from hand to hand, calling, "I think we should stop for the day. It's gotten really hot out."

"I'm fine, so don't you worry about me," Alice returned, giving a weak laugh. Her loose skirts, which had felt so light earlier, now encumbered her every step. Dots lined her vision as she blinked against the glare. *So. . .hot.* She dropped her gaze to find, oddly enough, the lawn rising up to meet her. The cool grass crashed against her blazing cheek, and she sighed as the oppressive heat vanished from her thoughts.

Feeling something entirely different than the soft lawn, Alice became very aware of a linen fabric against her cheek that was *moving.* With a cry, she opened her eyes to find herself in Giles's arms and being carried toward the big house. "I'm so sorry," she murmured, pushing against his thick shoulder.

"No, I should be the one apologizing. I should have listened to my better judgment and stopped us when it grew too hot, but I wished to please you," he replied, misery exuding from his every word.

His kindness made her throat swell with suppressed emotion. How long had it been since a man tried to do something sweet just to please her? She dared to lay a hand on his broad chest, staying him for a moment as his brilliant eyes met her own, and she couldn't bring herself to ask him to set her down. "Thank you, but I'm quite well now. Would you mind taking me home?"

"As long as you allow me to send the doctor to attend to you there if you won't have him here," Giles countered.

"I promise you, I am fine." She felt his tense shoulders relax.

"Very well, but I am seeing you into your

shop, and if your assistant is present, up to your second-floor landing, no matter how much you protest."

She laid her cheek against his chest once more. "Deal."

CHAPTER SEVEN

Alice's shoulders sagged as she packed away her sewing supplies while Constance rushed down to host her first dinner party as a married woman, a fact that she mentioned at least three times in the space of a half hour. She rubbed her hand over her face, exhausted from being called out for a fitting emergency just when she was sitting down to her hot dinner. She wrapped her light shawl about her shoulders and took the servant's exit as disappointment filled her over not seeing Giles.

Ever since their match five days ago that ended without a dinner invitation, she'd been thinking about him constantly and had been trying to think of a way to see him again without coming across as desperate. So when the freshly returned Mrs. Eustace Merrick sent a servant with a message regarding a too-tight bodice, she had eagerly complied for a chance to see Giles, only to be crushed to learn from Constance that he worked late most nights.

Stepping out into the heavy evening air, she was surprised to see it had grown so dark. Alice squinted to read her watch pin. She must've been in the mansion longer than she thought. She bit her lip, craning her neck toward the stables, hoping to see a carriage ready to bring her home, but there had been no mention of the Claytons' buggy taking her home and there wasn't a groomsman waiting for her.

Alice checked her handbag and grimaced. In her haste to possibly see Giles, she had forgotten her purse along with her coin for a hired carriage, but even if she had remembered, money was too dear to waste on a three-mile carriage ride home when she could just as easily walk. She clutched her bag, straightened her shoulders, and strode down the sidewalk as quickly as she could, praying that the coarse sailors who daily swarmed to Charleston's port would not be bothering her tonight. Once on King Street and in the glow of the gas streetlights, she picked up her pace, eager for her now-cold dinner, a pot of tea, and her magazine.

Her pulse quickened when two sailors from across the street at a public house caught sight of her, one pointing in her direction. Keeping her chin lifted in a confident manner, she strode onward, passing the pub and its cacophony of bawdy music. She had just as much a right to be out on the street as any man. She was dressed as a lady, and if these roguish-looking men did not treat her as one, they would soon find out that she was no damsel. Reaching into her valise, her fingers wrapped around her steel scissors and, gripping the handle like a knife, she held them at the ready as she strode home. Footsteps sounded behind her and at first she pretended to ignore them, praying they did not belong to the two staring men. *Almost there.*

But when their rakish laughter and crude

comments reached her ears, she twirled around, pursed her lips, and narrowed her eyes. In a firm voice, she commanded, "I suggest you step away from me and mind your tongue. You come near me, and you'll be sorry you ever approached me." She withdrew her scissors from her bag, the freshly sharpened blades catching in the gaslights. She glared at the sailors. She had worked twelve hours and would put up with nothing. The men did not even blink at her scissors. They laughed even louder and continued to approach her. Alice began to reconsider her stance of holding her ground and stumbled backward a few paces, her arm still poised, ready to stab if necessary. "Back off now."

"Looks like we have a fighter." The red-bearded man elbowed his taller companion.

"Good. I like a bit of a challenge. Come on, girly. You wouldn't have walked by here unless you wanted us to buy you a drink."

She hated that she could not keep the tremor out of her voice. "I've warned you. I *will* hurt you."

The men grinned and the red-bearded

sailor lunged for her, knocking her bag to the ground, scattering her precious silk threads and silver engraved thimble. In a single, swift motion, she shrieked and jammed the point of her scissors into the shoulder of her assailant. He cried out as she twisted the scissors and jerked them out and gave the tall sailor a swift kick to the shin, picking up her skirts to make a run for it. But the tall man caught her by her full sleeve, ripping it and baring her shoulder. *Dear Lord, help me.* She shoved her elbow into his nose and screamed. "Help!" His filthy fingers grasped at her waist as she tripped and cried out for help again, scrambling to her feet.

A gentleman in formal attire thrust himself between them and rammed his fist into the tall man's jaw, sending the thug staggering backward. "Did they hurt you, Alice?"

"Giles," she gasped, nearly in tears at the sight of him. Retrieving her scissors from the ground, she turned to find the red-bearded man rallying as the tall sailor snatched a log from a pile of firewood beside the bakery.

With his attention on the red-bearded man, Giles didn't see the other draw up the log like a club, his gaze on Giles's head. Alice screamed a warning, and Giles dodged, directly into the second man's fist. Giles went sprawling as Alice shoved the red-bearded man back to ground, taking care to hit his arm where she had wounded him and making him howl in pain.

Giles wiped his forehead with the back of his hand and, seeing blood, laughed, rising to his feet and pushing his sleeves up. He lifted his fists, the veins in his athletic forearms cording with power. "That was a mistake."

The tall man gripped the jacket collar of his injured friend and hoisted him up, scrambling away. "Come on before someone sends for the police. No skirt is worth a beating."

Before she knew what she was about, Alice dropped her scissors and flung herself into Giles's strong arms, ducking her head into his chest, the tears clogging her throat as she whimpered his name over and over.

GILES'S HEART stumbled at the closeness of her. He wrapped his arms about her and laid his chin atop her hair that held the faint scent of gardenias, ignoring the throbbing pain in his jaw and relishing the tender moment until he heard a sniff. He pulled back, his hands on her arms, reluctant to release her for even a moment. "Are you hurt?"

She shook her head, using her lace cuff to dab at her cheeks. He retrieved a cotton handkerchief from his pocket and pressed it into her hand.

Alice turned her back to him, affording herself a bit of privacy. "Thank you. I don't know what I would've done if you hadn't shown up. I'm so thankful you happened to be near."

"And I. Though, I have to say you were doing quite well without any assistance." Giles swiped at his chin with the sleeve of his jacket, not caring that his sister would raise a fuss over the state of his clothes. He would have words with Constance for sending Alice out in the darkness without even a thought of how she would return home. When he had discovered at dinner that Alice had come and gone into the night, he had left the party without a word, jogging down the streets looking for her when he heard a scream that struck him to the core.

He reached out, daring to gently stroke her cheek with the back of his hand at the memory. Giles shuddered to think what could have happened, and he was thankful that Alice had the presence of mind to withdraw her scissors from her bag to defend herself. Thinking of her scissors, he bent down and scooped them off the ground and wiped them against his black pant leg. She protested. "Don't! You'll ruin—"

But he had already smeared a dark stain across his pant leg. "Looks like you winged one of them pretty good."

"I wish I'd winged both of them." She straightened her hat, the poor decorative bird atop looking like it had seen better days, and examined her ripped sleeve. "Thankfully, I can fix this, but I can't say the same for my new hat." She looked up to his forehead, concern etched in her eyes. "Giles, you could have been seriously injured. . .and I couldn't forgive myself if something happened to you on my account."

His brows rose. "So, you finally admit it. You *do* care for me."

She gave him that dimpled smile that sent his heart skipping. "Why else would I be staying after our lessons for half an hour for the past month during busy season?"

He grinned, unable to contain his joy. "I've been thinking about you all week."

"Oh? Have you now?"

He tucked a strand of fiery hair behind her ear. "Yes. I've been thinking of the perfect excuse to come see you all week."

She lifted her brow and sheepishly returned his grin. "My excuse was to come running the second your family beckoned even though it was dinnertime and I had bought a delicious-smelling meat pie from the bakery across the street." She spoke so quietly he barely heard her as they walked toward her shop, but her confession gave him the courage to admit his own plans.

"Well, I thought about breaking my pocket watch to visit the clock shop next door and magically run in to you, or losing Constance's favorite set of gloves prior to the dinner party, but those excuses all seemed too fabricated." *And I wanted our next meeting to be a little bit more romantic.* He paused at her doorway and leaned against the frame, waiting there while she opened the shop, entered, and lit a lamp. "Alice, it's been a month and I still haven't changed my mind," he said when she rejoined him at the door.

She lifted her lamp and gasped. "Giles! Your face is bleeding yet. Come in, and I'll dress it."

He regarded the empty, dark room and thought of her reputation. "I'm not sure if that is the best idea."

"We will stay downstairs by the window with the lamp glowing for all the world to see, so we won't truly be alone. I'm more worried about you passing out in the street from blood loss than my own reputation at the moment."

"I will on one condition." He gave her a half grin.

"What's that?"

"You allow me to take you to dinner tomorrow night. It's the least I can do since Constance spoiled your meat pie," he added with a wink.

She rolled her eyes and waved him inside. "You are incorrigible. Fine. Now, let me attend to your wound." She pulled him inside and set him on a stool in front of the shop window before ducking into the back and returning, balancing a basin of water that sloshed onto her skirt, another lamp, and a basket of what appeared to be medical supplies. "My assistant isn't as experienced with using the Singer sewing machine as I am and, well, running the needle over one's fingers can leave quite the mess." She pressed a clean, plain white handkerchief to the mouth of the amber bottle and flipped it over, allowing the liquid to seep into the cloth.

He inhaled sharply as she pressed the

cloth to his forehead. His racing pulse from the fight must have distracted him from the cut on his forehead. . .until now.

"Does it hurt?"

"Not as badly as sewing my finger, I'd imagine."

"I'm sorry. I wish I could be gentler, but I can't keep the witch hazel from stinging." She lightly patted the wound with the handkerchief, dipped it into the water, and dabbed his head again. "Thank you for rescuing me. And just so you know, I would have said yes without the bribe."

"And that is the best medicine a man could ever want." He caught her slender hand in his, tempted to press a kiss on her fingertips. Giles wanted to state his intentions to marry her then and there, but he didn't think his declaration would be well received just yet, given her uncertainty with even meeting with him after that disastrous encounter with Eustace. And despite his best efforts, Giles couldn't stanch his lingering desire to know why she was so hostile to Eustace. Her past didn't matter to him, but he felt like it would help him better understand her. "Do you mind terribly if I ask what happened the day of my sister's wedding? Why did Merrick look as if he had seen a ghost?"

Alice sucked in her cheeks as she wrapped the gauze around his head, and he grew afraid that he might have asked something from which there was no return. But as she pinned the bandage into place, her indigo eyes met his, and he could read a sadness behind them.

"I suppose it is only fair for you to understand what a risk you are taking by even being seen with me." She leaned against the counter and crossed her arms as she kicked at a bit of ivory thread on the hardwood floor. "I knew Eustace Merrick by another name, a name he abandoned after— But, I am getting ahead of myself. Eustace *Burke* was an apprentice in my father's shop for two years. When he started, I was merely an overgrown girl of sixteen, gangly, and irrevocably in love with him. He, of course, did not notice me until my eighteenth birthday, when I grew into my limbs."

He swallowed at her bluntness, watching

an alluring blush creep into her cheeks as she admitted this. *How could Eustace not have noticed such a beauty in all those years? I would have noticed you long before for your sweet spirit.*

"Our romance was forbidden by Father, and that made it all the more desirable for Eustace, I believe. When Father discovered us stealing a kiss inside the workshop when Eustace was supposed to be working, my father realized that prohibiting our love had done nothing to keep us apart. Reluctantly, he gave us his blessing, and Eustace and I were engaged and planned to wed shortly after my nineteenth birthday once the rush of the season was over and my dearest friend Meg had returned from her finishing school abroad."

She gave a short, bitter laugh. "To thank Father for his blessing, I designed a lovely, intricate quilt made from the material of a few of my mother's gowns, an old vest that he used to wear for special occasions, and a childhood dress or two of mine. I wanted to show Father that even though I was getting married—" She pressed her hand to her mouth and shook her head. "But, of course, that never happened. I almost burned it, but the memories it held were so dear that I just packed it away."

"And that's how Meg never knew Merrick was actually your"—Giles had never hated the words more—"*former* fiancé. He had ended things before she returned home."

She nodded. "Exactly."

Giles didn't want to think of Eustace stealing Alice's kisses or breaking her heart, but he had to know. "What stopped the two of you from marrying?"

"The thing that keeps most marriages from occurring. Even though Eustace said he loved me and I imagined myself in love with him and we had the most blissful courtship, it wasn't strong enough to withstand—" She dipped her head and wiped her eyes, laughing. "I don't know why I'm crying. It's been years since the scandal."

His heart stopped. The circumstances must have been truly horrible for a man to breach his promise and not worry about repercussions. But Giles remained silent and waited for her to speak.

"Days after our engagement, it was discovered that Father had been stealing from one of his clients. Or, rather, he had been caught by only one. He later confided to me that he had taken from a couple other clients, but had done so in ways that they did not notice or suspect him. A little here and a little there. But then we had an exceptionally poor month in the shop, and Father risked stealing a valuable antique vase." She swallowed. "He hoped for leniency from the judge and told me not to worry. However, it turned out that the worth of the vase he had stolen was far greater than he had originally told me. The court investigated, and I was shocked to discover the extent of my father's theft, which, as you can guess, went beyond the few clients that he had confessed to me."

"Oh Alice." He ran his hand over the back of his neck. *No wonder she is so enigmatic and untrusting. She's ashamed of her father's actions and lies.*

"Apparently, he had been lining his

pockets with bills or items from people's houses with little consequence to himself for *years*. Multiple servants appeared in court, proclaiming they had been released from their positions without references on the accusation of theft brought on by Father's actions." Her voice cracked. "Many of the servants had families who depended on them, and the judge did not look kindly on Father profiting from his wealthy clients at the expense of modest servants. The judge condemned my father to twenty years' hard labor." She looked up at Giles, her fists clenched. "And he deserved every year he received."

Giles reached for her hand, his fingers encasing hers for only a moment before she stepped back from him and set to work putting away her supplies. "But you managed to keep the shop," he ventured, hoping to pull her from her dark memories to something he knew she loved.

"Yes. Only just. The judge was kind to me. Instead of seizing all my father's assets and turning me into a homeless pauper, he said I could keep a small percentage of whatever I sold from the shop and apply the rest to debts until they were paid in full."

"But I'm assuming Eustace was not as understanding?" Giles watched her carefully.

She gave a short laugh and set the basket under the counter, her hands trembling as she flattened them against the front of her skirt. "Eustace said my father's scandal would be the death of his career if word circulated that he was somehow connected with Turner's Fine Tailor, and he certainly could not be connected to it through a marriage with the thieving scoundrel's daughter. I begged Eustace not to leave me, but after the ruling, he abandoned me on the courthouse steps with almost nothing to my name and no one to share my burden. He had promised to love and protect me, but when it came right down to it, Eustace would only love and protect himself. He left me and evidently changed his name. I changed the tailor shop's name to Thimbles and Threads Bridal Shop and never looked back. It took me five years of backbreaking toil to work myself out of Father's debts and to build a name for myself. This past year was the first time I was able to hire an assistant and finally earn some high society patrons." She straightened her shoulders. "And, my friend, that brings us to the wedding last month."

Giles clenched his jaw, ignoring the pain and wishing he could wring Eustace's neck for abandoning Alice all those years ago. No wonder she had been so reluctant to allow him into her life. Every man she had ever trusted had let her down in a colossal way. His throat tightened as he realized that she had been so crushed by men that she didn't even bother to name her cat anything other than "Cat" for fear that he would one day leave her too. Giles rose, taking her shoulders in his hands. "But I am not like them." *I would never abandon you.*

She gave him a stiff smile and a laugh that cracked with suppressed emotion. "You say that now, but your family would never accept me, and if they didn't—"

"You seem to forget that my father is only a banker because my grandfather married well and worked his way up to buy the bank." He gave her a sad smile. "And we already have a tailor in the family through Constance's marriage. It's not a stretch for us to court. Alice, you *know* me. . .possibly better than anyone ever has. You know I would never do that to you."

She rested her fingers on his, stroking his tan knuckles. "I know you wouldn't," she whispered, her long lashes fairly brushing her rosy freckled cheeks. "You are too kind to ever hurt a woman like that." She lifted her hands from his. "You are a good friend, Giles."

"For being so clever, how could you not realize by now how much I care for you *beyond* friendship?" He cupped her cheek in his hand and tilted her face up to his. "How could you not know that I think of you from the moment I open my eyes to the moment I close them to dream of you? Since I've met you, every beat of my heart is for you, my Alice. Won't you take the chance to fall in love with me? Let me court you. Allow me the chance to gain your trust and your heart." His eyes settled on her lips and, as she said nothing, he leaned forward, his lips a breath away from hers when she pulled back, nearly tripping over her skirts.

"The hour is quite late. You'd best be on your way, else your family will think something happened."

Giles prayed he had not been too forward, but then she rose on her tiptoes and lightly kissed him on the cheek.

"I'll think on it, but until then, be content with dinner tomorrow night."

CHAPTER EIGHT

Alice dropped another gardenia that was meant for her hair. Her fingers could not stop trembling. She had expected to feel relieved after having shared her burden with someone after so many years. She drew a ragged breath as her stomach twisted. *How could I have allowed myself to be caught up in the emotion of the moment and risk my shop's reputation?* One word from Giles could remind her clients of her shop's less than desirable beginnings. She gripped the corners of her vanity, her head sagging, and gathered her rising panic. She knew he would never purposely harm her or her business. And yet, his sister was an influential client. If he inadvertently let it slip to someone who'd never approve of their relationship, Alice would be ruined. She shook her head to banish her train of thought that would only end catastrophically. She knew him. Giles was not like Eustace. He was not like Father. She straightened her shoulders and finished dressing her hair. She would not allow her past to mar the present.

She stared into the looking glass and saw in front of her a stylish woman in a silk russet skirt with so many tucks in the bustle, it caught on every piece of light, making it glisten. She adjusted the lace on her soft, pearl-white sleeves, satisfied that in every visible sense of the word, she appeared to be a lady of refinement. She turned, admiring the tucks and twists of her gown, and sighed. If only forging a new heritage was as easy as assembling a new wardrobe. Giles's family would never approve of her scandalous past, and the little money she had finally set aside was hardly enough to lure a fine gentleman into overlooking said past. *Stop it.* She kicked at the soiled blossom on the floor and plucked another gardenia from the vase, tucking it into place and enjoying the sweet perfume the white flower offered her ensemble.

Glancing at her watch pin atop her dresser, Alice grabbed her footed crystal hand lamp and decided she had just enough time to finish the last bit of embroidery on the bodice of a bridesmaid gown she had been working on earlier. She settled downstairs at her station, hoping to lose herself in her work, but with every stitch, she thought of him. *Be honest, Alice. The real reason you are so torn over tonight's dinner is because you allowed yourself to grow close to him and are deathly afraid of something happening to him or having to live through another heartbreak.*

She snapped off the ends of the blush-colored thread as if it were her relationship with Giles, doomed to be cut short. She shook the dress free of threads and, satisfied that she had finished the hardest parts, set it on the back of her assistant's chair as the clock shop next door sounded the time, chiming a cheerful six o'clock. As if on cue, Giles's buggy for two rolled to a halt in front of her shop. She watched Giles hop down from the buggy in a plain navy suit and she ran her hand over her bodice, thankful he had told her to wear a visiting gown in place of a dinner dress. Even though it seemed odd, it lent an air of mystery to their outing that she quite fancied. She wrapped her embroidered silk shawl about her shoulders and stepped outside, locking the shop and dropping the key into her beaded reticule.

"Good evening, my lady." Giles bowed, pressing his stiff hat over his heart. "Are you up for an evening drive?"

"Certainly. It will be nice to spend more than a few minutes of my day outside," she replied as the lavender and blush sunset cast a glow about them. She placed her hand in his and allowed him to whisk her away into the unknown of the evening. "You seem to be healing quickly."

"Well, when my family saw my cuts, they sent for the doctor at once." He laughed. "You would think I'd never taken a blow before. They should have seen me in London when I attempted to teach this one young lord. He smashed my face with the racket at just the perfect angle to break my nose. The beautiful creature you see in front of you today is nothing short of a miracle. If there hadn't been a doctor at the courts when it happened, I'm sure my nose would've been ruined for life."

She laughed at his bravado and dared to admire his strong jawline and profile as he pointed out each bit of scenery in passing as if she were a tourist. She enjoyed playing along and trusting him with the evening's events. They turned onto East Battery, and the wind picked up as it flowed over the waves, drawing her attention to the harbor and the island of Fort Sumter in the middle. A gust slammed into her, sending her perfect coiffure into a riotous mess.

Giles sent her an apologetic smile. "Sorry about the wind, but I thought you'd enjoy the harbor view for a moment. I know how much you like being near water."

She blushed at his thoughtfulness, stunned that he remembered that tiny detail from one of their first conversations together. She laughed to distract him from noticing her heightened color and gripped the side of the buggy, the gardenias in her hair perilously loose. "While I do, I think perhaps the river might be our best hope for a water view since it is so windy tonight?"

"I'm glad you suggested that." Giles grinned as if he knew something she didn't and turned them down a street, headed in the opposite direction of the harbor. For the next quarter of an hour, they conversed on every topic *but* her confession of last night, and when they turned into his drive, her heart nearly pounded out of her chest.

"You can't be taking me to dinner at your house with your family?" she squeaked. Her hands flew to her hair, which she knew was a tangled mess. "And I'm not dressed for a formal dinner! You specifically said in your note—"

"Oh no, I wouldn't do that to you. We won't even be going in the house," he reassured her. "Besides, Father, Constance and, uh, her husband are all away this evening having dinner at William and Meg's new townhouse." He directed the gig off the main road and onto what appeared to be a wide walking path, jostling their shoulders together with each turn of the wheel.

"No need to avoid mentioning Eustace's name on my account," she replied, holding up her hand. "I have long since moved past him and feel no hurt at the mention of his name." *Though the sight of him turns my stomach.*

"Good. Though I'm afraid it may take me a bit longer to get over his treatment of you."

Turning the corner, Alice gasped at the sight of the riverboat on the Ashley River, bedecked with what seemed to be nearly a hundred candles surrounding a small table set for two on the promenade deck.

"I thought you might enjoy a peaceful evening on the river and possibly a river cruise after dinner?" He hopped down and reached up for her. "That's why I suggested a visiting gown, so you'd have sleeves to keep the mosquitos at bay."

"I wondered." She giggled, feeling lighter than she had in years. As it was too far for her to jump, she surrendered to him, allowing him to wrap his hands about her waist and gently lift her from the buggy to the ground. He didn't set her down but instead cradled her in his arms.

"Giles!" She gave a nervous laugh, glancing back to the house.

"The ground is still soggy from that heavy rain this morning," he explained, taking the pathway lit with lanterns to the riverboat where a couple of servants awaited them and a handful of men that she assumed were the pilot and crew, judging from their attire.

Her cheeks burned at being seen in such a manner, but she gave them a nod and attempted to smile with dignity as she said through gritted teeth, "Okay, you can set me down now."

Giles laughed, the small charming space in his front teeth making him even more endearing. "Your wish is my command."

With her feet set firmly on the worn floorboards of the riverboat, she gathered her skirts and followed him up the riverboat's stairs to the promenade deck. In the flickering candlelight against the last rays of the sunset, Alice was taken with the beauty of the swamp surrounding her, the croaking of the frogs, the gray moss fluttering in the light breeze as the boat swayed ever so slightly in the current of the lazy Ashley River. She peered over the edge of the rail to spy five turtles scuttle off a fallen log and plop into the green film resting atop the dark waters. She grinned as the smallest finally managed to wriggle off its resting place to join its family. Lulled by the splendor, she lifted her gaze to Giles, her breath catching at the expression on his face, captured in the light of a hundred candles.

GILES WAS TAKEN with her exquisiteness, her delight with small creatures. His sister never took the time to stare over the railing once she had her sights set on higher things, like a husband with a fortune. He joined her by the rail and observed the river through Alice's eyes. He had long since taken the riverboat for granted as an extension of his home, but he had to admit that it was quite a luxury. He was struck by the thought that unlike him, she had worked for everything that she owned. Admiration for her passion turned his gaze to her. Surrendering any pretense of being discreet, he openly studied the curve of her lips. His gaze finally rested on her wide eyes, and he knew he would never take her for granted should she ever trust her hand to him. "Alice, I've enjoyed our time together and—"

"Me too." She cut him off as if afraid of what he might say.

"While we've only been acquainted for almost two months, I want you to know my intent—"

"Oh, is that dinner I smell? I'm starving." She grabbed his arm, steering him toward the table as dinner was indeed being served. She nodded to the butler and, without waiting for Giles to assist her, she slipped into her chair and opened her napkin with a snap. She then lifted a crystal glass of water to her lips, her gaze drifting toward the stars.

Giles wished to press the topic, but from the way she fairly jumped into the river to shy away from him, he knew it was too soon. Yet part of him felt that if he did not declare his intentions, he was being as dishonorable as Eustace Merrick.

Alice directed their conversation to a humorous encounter with a client, tennis, and even spoke of her childhood as if to distract him from the topic on his heart. They were nearing the end of their meal when a few lamps bobbing in the distance seemed to be approaching the river along the path coming from—*the house*! He groaned and looked to Alice, who was finishing off her chocolate cake with such enthusiasm that he would have laughed if not for the impending doom of their dinner.

"I saw the riverboat from the house and I wondered what possibly could be happening. What on earth are you doing with all those lamps and candles? Are you trying to set the swamp ablaze?" Constance stepped from the dock and up the gangplank, waving away the servant escorting her with two lamps.

Giles pressed his lips into a thin line, certain that the servants informed his sister that he was entertaining a young lady and she couldn't keep herself from marching down to find out who it was. He had purposefully not told anyone who his guest was so as not to draw attention to Alice. He knew how she detested being in the spotlight. His gaze darted to Alice, and he saw that her hands were busy twisting her napkin in her lap.

"Giles," she whispered through her smile as Constance's footsteps sounded on the stairs leading up to the decks. "You said they were gone!"

"Did he?" Constance's brow quirked and her gaze settled on Alice as her mouth formed a disapproving line, all politeness banished from her eyes. "No wonder you were so secretive. You wanted to have your dalliance with our seamstress without interference."

Giles frowned as he rose with Alice. "Constance! You forget yourself."

Alice slowly wiped her lips free of any trace of chocolate. "Well, that was a delicious meal, and I thank you, Giles, but I'm afraid that the hour is quite late and I must be on my way."

"I quite agree with you." Constance's raven manufactured curls bobbed as she gave Alice a pert nod.

"Alice, it is hardly eight o'clock. We were supposed to go on a river cruise."

Her gaze darted to his sister. "Not tonight, I'm afraid. I remembered that I have some work to see to that cannot wait."

"Nonsense. You promised me an evening in payment of my near-death experience." He half-heartedly teased, but Constance had ruined any chance he had of telling Alice his intentions.

She backed away, sending her chair tumbling to its side.

"I'm sorry. This was a mistake." She moved for the stairs, nodding to his sister. "Miss Constance, I hope you won't change your mind about using me in the future."

"You can bet your bustle that I will no longer use your services, and I will be sure to spread the word among your clients that you *flirt* with your employers in an attempt to ensnare a rich husband."

"Constance, be quiet. You have no idea what you are talking about." Giles stepped forward, wishing he could place a protective arm about Alice but knowing it would not be welcome.

Constance pursed her lips. "I am quite decided that Miss Turner will *never* work for any other decent bride in the future."

"But Mrs. Merrick, I—" Alice's voice cracked as his sister waved her along.

"I will not be moved. Imagine a *seamstress* going after one of my brothers." She shook her head, lip curling in disgust.

"You seem to forget, Constance, about our own heritage." Giles had expected a little resistance, but to have his sister be so blatantly rude to Alice was not to be borne. "And not to mention the obvious, but you happened to be *married* to a tailor."

She sniffed and lifted her chin. "Eustace is *successful* and wants to further himself. He dreams of becoming far more than his simple tailor beginnings, as you can see from his business growth. The difference between Eustace and this sad excuse for a designer is night and day."

"Constance." He clenched his fists. "Apologize to Miss Turner at once."

"I will not. Eustace told me everything about her past. She is nothing more than the girl who stopped at nothing to trap Eustace into an engagement, so you best rid yourself of this seductress!"

Alice picked up her skirts and fled down the stairs and toward the gangplank. Giles sent his sister a glare and trotted after Alice. He would have words with Constance later.

"Wait! Alice!" He hurried down the path, reaching for her elbow. "You can't just go running off into the dark. This is a swamp. Do you want to be eaten? There are alligators just waiting for a chocolate-filled treat to come along the path."

She swatted at her neck. "Too late. The mosquitos seem to have found me at last."

"Are you that eager to be away from me that you would risk swamp fever and life and limb?"

"You don't understand." Her voice cracked and he could see her tears pooling. "I have worked for *years* to build my reputation, and in a single night, it is all gone."

"I'll take care of Constance. I'll explain

that you didn't want to come. That I bribed you."

She jerked her elbow out of his hand and wiped at her cheeks, her gaze hardening. It was as if he could see the walls that had taken him weeks to dismantle go up again and rise even higher. "I need to go."

"I'll take you home," he replied, seeing that there was no way they could speak while she was so angry. "I'm so sorry for what Constance said to you. There is no excuse for her to treat you as she did, and I will let her know."

She drew a deep breath and smoothed her russet skirt. "She may have been rude, but she reminded me of why dinner with you was a mistake. Can you have one of your staff take me home?"

Her request throbbed more than taking a racket to the face. "If you wish."

"I do."

CHAPTER NINE

Alice inhaled sharply through her teeth and jerked her hand away from the offending needle. She wrapped her finger in a handkerchief and set to work again on the intricate embroidery on the collar of a wedding dress, minding her needle this time. She could not afford to stain the cloth by her carelessness.

"Giles is here to see you, *again,*" Meg called from around the thick curtain separating the workroom from the front of the shop.

"I'm busy."

"You've said that every day for six days. My new brother-in-law is in misery. It is obvious he is not just some dandy trying to—"

Alice sent her a glare. "I thought you came for a visit, not a lecture."

"Fine." Meg lifted her hands in surrender and spoke softly to Giles before the front door slammed, sending the copper bell jingling in protest.

She hardened her spirit. She could not risk being seen with Giles. So far, business continued as usual. Constance hadn't exposed the secret dinner rendezvous, but that didn't mean she wouldn't if she felt that Alice was trying to steal her brother's affections. But Alice had long since buried that dream of becoming a bride when Eustace had left her. And she had worked too long and too hard to have it taken from her by a spoiled, overgrown girl.

"When are you going to speak to him?" Meg reclined on the ratty settee that Alice only kept to take naps on if she needed to work late and was too tired to venture up the stairs. Meg selected an oatmeal cookie from the china plate and dabbed her forehead with the corner of her handkerchief.

"You skipped your tennis lesson and you *never* do that, not even after what happened at my wedding. I've never seen you as happy as you have been since meeting that wonderful brother-in-law of mine."

"It is as hot as a frying pan this week. You can't expect me to play in this heat." She ducked her head before the real reason could tumble out.

Meg traced the edge of her cookie, causing some of the oats to shed into her lap as she brooded. "It hurts me to think you were in so much pain that day and I didn't even know."

"I wasn't about to ruin your day with my bit of nonsense from the past." She dropped her sewing into her lap and looked to her most trusted friend. "What would you have me do, Meg? If I don't cut Giles out of my life, I risk losing everything. . .for potentially nothing. How can I trust him with my heart after everything I've been through?"

Meg lowered her treat and reached out for Alice's hand. "But think of all you stand to gain if you let down your guard. You know I was afraid to surrender my independence to a man, but when I met William. . ." Meg gave her a half smile and shrugged. "I didn't give it a second thought, because he proved himself to be a true man of the Lord. You have spent enough time with Giles to know where his heart dwells. And I think you know where yours belongs."

The copper bell clanged again and, peering around the curtain to spy the back of a gentleman as he entered and examined the window display, Alice stepped out from her workshop. "Welcome to Thimbles and Threads Bridal Shop. How can I help you, sir?"

The customer turned to her, sending her heart stammering. "You can help me by keeping away from Giles Clayton. He is intended to marry Miss Castle, and you best guard yourself before he takes advantage of you in your vulnerable state. I heard from Miss Castle herself that they will be engaged by Christmas."

She gripped the counter at Eustace's announcement, but gathering herself, she pointed him to the door, her finger steady.

"You have no right to bid me do anything. I suggest you leave."

He stepped toward her, lust flickering in his eyes. "I always did like it when you pretended to stand up to me."

"I'm warning you, Eustace. I'm not a weak little girl anymore, ready to crumple under your will. Get out of my shop or I'll have the police throw you in prison for trespassing."

"And who would the police believe? A successful married gentleman, or a spinster seamstress desperate to save her shop after her father stole thousands?"

"The spinster." Meg appeared, her eyes narrowing at Eustace. "If you wish to continue living at Clayton Plantation with our father-in-law, I suggest you take your leave. I'm certain he would not look kindly on the man who broke his only daughter's heart when news of a scandalous tête-à-tête begins circulating Charleston, which is what will happen should you falsely accuse Alice of anything, *brother*."

Taken aback, Eustace's bravado wavered and in that moment, Alice brushed past him and threw open the shop door, banging it against the wall. "Don't *ever* come back."

GILES HAMMERED ball after ball over the net in the last bit of light, desperate for a distraction from his thoughts. He had sent notes, bouquets, chocolates, and come in person countless times to her shop, but everything returned to him untouched. He could pursue Alice all he wanted, but if she didn't even open the door for him. . . He squeezed the grip of the racket, grunting as his tennis ball bounced into the gardens, yards from where he had been aiming.

Lord, please let me not have pushed her away. I would never do to her what Eustace and her father did. Help me to understand the depth of her hurt. He tossed another ball up and slammed it with his racket. *But how am I supposed to apologize to her or get her to trust me if she won't even speak to me? I should have stood up for her more than just a light scolding to my sister. I should've—*

"So, I heard from Constance that you

were having quite the clandestine meeting with my Alice." Eustace Merrick stumbled down the veranda steps, his hair askew.

Giles scowled at the man who had ruined his chance with Alice. "Drink some coffee, Merrick."

"Don't have to. The ladies will be gone for the rest of the evening. Some nonsense about dinner on the riverboat with their lady friends. No husbands."

"Don't you have a business to run?"

Merrick laughed. "When you are as successful as I am, you have people who run the business for you and you just reap the profits." He reached the net and leaned against the pole. "So, tell me, has Alice become less of a prude with age?"

Giles clenched his racket and sucked in a breath, hoping to suppress his rage, but Merrick uttered an unforgivable assumption and snorted.

"You will retract your statement, else I will forget that you are married to my sister."

Merrick picked up a racket, a gleam in his eyes as he ran a finger over the frame.

"You keep away from Alice, and I might consider it."

Giles scowled. "I repeat, *sir*, you are *married* to my sister. I do not think it is appropriate for you to forbid me to see any woman, especially not one you abandoned five years ago."

"So that little minx told you? Well, since we are brothers, as you keep reminding me, I don't think a brother should court another man's previous fiancée."

"I don't know what my sister ever saw in you."

"The same thing Alice did." He grinned. "Now, I'll ask nicely one more time."

ALICE COULDN'T BRING herself to go to bed quite yet. She decided to treat herself to a pot of herbal tea and the last of the oatmeal cookies from the bakery over a *Harper's Bazaar*. Not bothering to undress, she unfastened and kicked off her shoes, pushed back the mosquito netting of her small four-poster bed, and nestled atop her lace bedspread, tucking her feet under herself. She held the magazine up to the lamplight, but the latest fashion designs did not stir her creativity as they usually did. Her mind kept drifting to Giles and Meg's assessment of her behavior. *Lord, am I mistaken in wanting to protect myself from being hurt again?*

Cat arched his back and darted across the room, upsetting the porcelain basin and nearly knocking it to the floor. "Cat!" Alice scrambled off the bed and flung open her bedroom door, shooing Cat down the stairs. A pounding at the front door of the shop made her heart jump. Her gaze flew to the clock on the mantel. *Half past nine? Who on earth would be calling at this late hour?* She bit her lower lip until she spied something that could be used as a weapon leaning against the armoire. Her fingers wrapped about her racket and, lifting it like a mace in one hand and the footed lamp in the other, she drew a ragged breath and descended the stairs, her stockinged feet silent on the wood floors. She squinted, unable to see who was at her shop door through the voile over the door's window. Setting her lamp on the front counter, she shouted, "Who is there?"

"It's me, Alice. You have to talk with me."

Even as her shoulders sagged with relief at the sound of Giles's voice, her stomach knotted. *I can't see him now.* Her hands flew to her hair only to remember she had already pulled the pins from her coiffure, allowing her curls to spill loosely to her waist. She leaned against the door, thankful for the sheer voile lending her a bit of privacy to gather herself. "Giles, I—"

"I promise I will leave the instant you've told me that you feel nothing for me."

I can't do the same thing that Eustace did to me. There one day and gone the next. . .not without telling him why. She grunted, unfastened the bolt, and cracked the door open enough to see his face, a bloodied mess.

"What on earth!" She jerked it open and pulled him inside. Her hands fluttered to her mouth as she took in his state. "Giles, what happened to you?"

He shrugged. "It's nothing."

"Nothing?" She scowled, shaking her head. She pushed his shoulder down, forcing him to take a seat. "You call this nothing? For a man who sits behind a desk every day, you sure do find the time to get into brawls every chance you can get."

"We all have our faults. Mine happens to be my temper when someone insults people I love."

Is he implying I am one of those people? She swallowed back the lump in her throat. "Who did this to you?"

He clenched his fists and looked to the ceiling. "With the ladies out for the night, Merrick took the opportunity to imbibe and come down to the lawn court to discuss—well—you."

"You fought with Eustace?" She pressed her hand to her lips, sick that Eustace may have ruined her life a second time.

Giles touched his head gingerly. "Merrick cracked a racket over my head before I knew we were fighting. Apparently, he's been stewing over my friendship with you and was jealous. I didn't want to retaliate, but the fool kept challenging me. When he charged at me again, I knocked him out in one punch that hopefully won't leave anything more than a bruised eye and pride."

Her jaw dropped. "Oh Giles. . ."

"I know you think that your family had problems, but seems like my family is just as imperfect, and that our mutual friend, Eustace, wants only what he cannot have." He shoved his hands into his pockets as she dripped water from the crystal pitcher she kept for guests onto her handkerchief and lifted it to his forehead. He tilted his head back. "There's not witch hazel on that cotton, is there? I'm already in enough pain." The crack in his lip turned his smile into a wince.

"Just water." She dabbed at his wound. Had it really only been a week since the last time she had bandaged his wounds? "You can't stay long. If someone walks by the shop and sees you in here *again*. . . There will be no benefit of the doubt given this time."

"I have to speak with you. Light the lamps like last time and turn up all the wicks to show that we are doing nothing wrong. We are chaperoned by every passerby."

She dropped her hand and stepped away from him, acutely aware for the first time that she was without shoes. "I'm afraid that I am causing too much of a stir in your family's lives. Please tell your sister to take her business to Miss Cole. She is quite the proficient seamstress."

"Alice. If you no longer wish to see me, please tell me, and I will leave you be, but you can't just ignore me and expect me to retreat without an explanation."

"What makes you think I'm cutting you out of my life?" She turned away from him and grabbed the broom, setting to cleaning the spotless showroom floor.

"Maybe because you can't even look at me. Or perhaps the dozens of returned messages."

She propped the broom against the counter, slowly turning to him. "You say you want to court me. You say that you would *never* hurt me, but how can you not hurt me if you do not plan on marrying me?" Her voice cracked.

"What?" He blinked, rising from his chair so quickly that he swayed.

She threw her arms around his waist, fearing he would pass out and further injure himself. He leaned into her arms, his breath on her hair.

"Why in the world would you think that?" he asked at last.

His question jarred her into thinking properly and she reluctantly slipped her arms from his side and stepped back. "Eustace came by today and told me that Miss Castle has implied you two are courting and are expected to wed soon."

"That is utter nonsense. My sister has been pushing me toward Miss Castle for years because they are best friends." He grasped her hand in his. "You have to believe me."

"I-I do," she whispered. "But that doesn't mean I can still see you. I'm too broken." She pressed a hand to her chest. "My heart was shattered the day my father left me, and I'm only now getting the pieces back. You deserve a heart that is whole and perfect."

He pressed a kiss onto each of her hands

with a pain in his eyes that wrenched her apart. "My sweet Alice. Don't you know that we are *all* imperfect beings? We are all broken. If you are searching for healing in your own strength, you will never find it. You've been running from men and your hurt for so long you seem to have forgotten from whom you are running. Mankind is broken. You know in your heart the only One who can make you whole again. Just stop your running and ask Jesus for healing." He stroked her cheek with his thumb. "He will bind your wounds and heal your heart if you only ask."

His words brought her to a halt. Had she really been leaning on herself for healing this entire time? *Dear Lord, forgive me.* Years of anger, fear, and bitterness began to crumble as his words burrowed into her heart. Tears filled her eyes and she dropped her gaze, convicted. Alice felt her body begin to shake, and she thought she was about faint when the pictures began tumbling off the walls. She whirled around to see the old brick chimney pull away from the wall and Giles in its direct path.

CHAPTER TEN

"Giles, it's an earthquake!" Alice shrieked and shoved him out of the way of the collapsing chimney. He wrapped his arms around her and, falling, rolling, they evaded the bricks slamming into the floorboards.

"We've got to get out of here before we're buried alive!" Giles pulled her up and they bolted for the door, but the upstairs floor began to crack and the floorboards rained down around them. With a yell, Giles pushed her against a wall that hadn't broken apart and formed a human cage around her, hunching his shoulders over her head to ensure that she would not be struck by the falling debris. "I've got you."

She looked up into his eyes that held protection and adoration. Knowing that this may be their last moments on earth together, she wrapped her arms around his neck and pressed her lips to his again and again, wincing against the debris hitting her hands. "I'm so sorry, Giles." Tears streamed down her face. *How could I have been so foolish to waste our precious time together because of my fears, my doubts. . . It doesn't matter now. All that matters is that I tell him before we die.* "I love you with all my heart."

For his answer, his lips sought hers again, but a board crashed into his shoulder, knocking him down into her. His startling look of peace calmed her as he answered, "My heart belonged to you the moment we met and forevermore, Alice Turner."

The walls trembled. *God help us,* she prayed as a bookcase filled with bridal accessories groaned and toppled toward them. She felt Giles's strong arms wrap around her again as he dived for the floor, appearing to be aiming for between the bookcase and the space between the counter and the floor. He tucked her head into his chest and let his shoulders take the brunt of the items tumbling out of the bookcase. The case slammed into the both of them but landed on the chimney rubble, saving them from being pinned to the floor. And with every violent tremor, Alice couldn't help but scream, clutching him.

Giles pressed a kiss atop her head. "If we get out of this alive, I'm going to ask you to marry me."

"If we get out of this alive, I'll say yes." She kissed his rough cheek. The house groaned again, and she screamed as something shattered on the bookcase and ash swirled about them.

THE THOUGHTS of Alice being his wife bolstered him even in the face of death. "It's all right. It's holding." Giles attempted to calm her, even though he had no assurance that they would be well or live to see another day. *Lord, You've brought us together.*

Please don't let our time together end so quickly. "Lord, please, protect us and our families. Stretch out Your mighty hand and make the earth grow still." He prayed aloud, cradling her as the tremors began to subside. He exhaled. *Thank You, Lord.* The quake had been the longest minute he'd ever experienced.

"Is it over?" she whispered, looking up to him, her face covered in ashes and dirt.

He loosened his grip on her and twisted to peek out from under the bookcase. "Hope so, but we better move before the aftershocks begin." He moved to position his shoulders under the bookcase and grunted as he stood, lifting it enough for them to slip out. "Go, Alice!"

She crawled out, and in a single motion, Giles shoved the bookcase off his shoulders and rolled out from under it, allowing it to crash on the rubble, splintering the already damaged wood, when the room began to shake again. Alice cried out and threw her arms around him as the aftershocks overtook the house and the things that had already shifted loose came tumbling down about them. Giles wrapped his arm around her waist and darted for the gaping hole in the wall, desperate to escape as a beam came crashing down, missing them by a hair-breadth.

Diving out onto the sidewalk, he held Alice against him. They lay panting on the ground, staring at the shop as flames began to lick the corner of her building. She pressed her hand to her mouth, staring in shock. Giles helped her to her feet and led her away from the shop and stood, along with the other merchants on King Street, in the middle of the road, watching the destruction as the hot, humid air hovered over them like a cloud. Giles laid his head atop her hair and held her close as screams escalated behind them and the darkness took on an amber glow. They turned to find the bakery across the street ablaze and the merchants next door to the bakery running in and out of the front door, trying to save merchandise as their wives in their dressing robes huddled with children in nightgowns at a safe distance.

Shaking, Alice rested her head on his chest. He felt her tears seep into his shirt as people began calling for their loved ones while others mourned the loss of their homes.

Thank You, Lord, that the women are on the river. Please let my family in Charleston be safe. He drew Alice's chin up to meet his starved gaze. "I mean it, Alice. If you'll have me, I want you to be my wife." He waited for her to raise questions, but instead, she offered him a tear-streaked smile.

"Everything you've done has proven you to be a man of your word. I know you do not ask me lightly or out of pity for my reduced circumstances." She laughed and gestured to her life's work in a heap. "You have waited for me to trust you, and I know I can. While every man in my life has left me, you are not every man. You are your own man, and you have my love."

His heart soared. "I half feared it was the terror of the moment that led you to confess your love."

She placed her hands in his. "Giles Clayton, I want to be your wife more than anything I've ever longed for in my entire life."

He gently cupped her face between his hands and kissed her. "Then be mine."

"Forever," she whispered, stepping into his embrace. Just then a guttural hiss sounded from the corner of her fallen home. They turned to find Cat, arching his back atop a small trunk on a heap that hadn't been eaten by the flames. "Cat! Oh Cat, you made it." She scooped up her black pet and buried her nose in its neck before looking down at the trunk. "I can't believe it. How did my parents' trunk survive?"

Stooping, she opened the lid and withdrew a half-finished quilt to reveal what appeared to be a wedding gown beneath. She stroked the quilt and looked up at Giles. "Life and love are too precious to squander over bitterness of past hurts. If you are willing, let's marry as soon as possible. Then I will work on this quilt, and when it is finished, I will deliver it to my father in person."

He knelt beside her, brushing his fingertips on her cheek. "Are you certain that this is what you want?"

She laughed. "My shop is in ruins and

the world is in chaos around us, but my heart has never been more at peace."

"We will rebuild again." He squeezed her hand. "Together."

Seeing that the merchants and their families about her were unharmed save for a few cuts, bruises, and the baker's broken leg, Giles held Cat in one arm, and with the trunk carried between them, they left her shop behind to find their family and friends to help in any way they could.

EPILOGUE

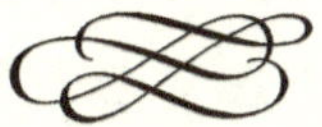

The days following the earthquake were filled with labor as everyone, rich and poor, attempted to piece their lives back together. Alice found that her assistant, Meg's family, and the Charleston jail had survived along with her father. Giles had word from his family that they were all alive and well. The number of fatalities overestimated in the newspapers lessened, but any number was still a tragedy felt by all survivors. Alice knew it would be a long time before their lives were mended and stitched back together, but with Giles by her side, she also knew for the first time in years that her burdens would be shared and her life would be full of love.

When Saturday arrived, Alice dressed in the only gown that survived the fire, her mother's wedding gown that spoke of blissful times gone by. In a simple ceremony, witnessed only by the preacher and his wife and Meg and William, Alice and Giles were married. And with their vows fresh on her lips, she stepped from the chapel with her husband at her side and her friends behind.

Husband. She sighed and rose on her tiptoes, pressing a kiss to his lips as their friends tossed handfuls of crimson rose petals into the air above them, calling out their congratulations.

"Giles! What on earth are you two about, kissing in the street?"

Alice felt her face turn crimson as she turned to find Giles's sister standing below them, mouth agape.

Constance's gaze fell to the gold band on Alice's finger and beyond to Meg and William. "Y-you didn't just get married, did you? I saw your note to Father and was coming to stop you. You couldn't have possibly gotten married without your entire family present."

"Dear sister, allow me to introduce you to my beautiful wife, Alice."

Her lips pursed. "Miss Turner, you took advantage of my brother during an emotional time. Despicable. And you, William, why didn't you talk some sense into him?"

Giles squeezed Alice's arm, silently reassuring her that *he* would fight this battle for them. "Constance, you know I love you, but it is not your place to say what is on my heart. Alice *is* my heart, and I won't stand by and allow you to disparage her. You cut her with your words and you in turn, cut me. Please don't ask me to choose between you."

She turned her fiery gaze from Giles to Alice and back before sighing. "I suppose there is no turning back now that you are married."

Giles reached for Alice's hand, wrapping it in a strong, firm grip. "No turning back. Not now, not ever."

Constance's shoulders slumped as she threw up her hands. "Fine. But, you'll have to give me some time to adjust to the idea of all this and not expect me to be all flowers and sunshine this morning."

"You? Not flowers and sunshine, my sister?" William chortled. "How uncharacteristic."

She cracked a smile and added, "But as I've always adored *you*, Giles, I'm sure I'll come around eventually for your sake, if for nothing else."

"Of course," Alice replied, understanding far more about the journey of forgiveness than her new sister-in-law knew.

"I suppose you'll be moving into the plantation too, with Father, Eustace, and me?"

"Actually, if you had read my message to Father through to the end, you would know of my plans for our living quarters. But I won't say what my plans are yet." He turned and grinned at Alice. "Because I wanted to surprise you. If you'll excuse us, Constance," he said, escorting Alice to his waiting buggy. And with a wave to their family, they wove down the streets toward the Ashley River, evading heaps of rubble and construction.

Spying the riverboat docked, she whirled to him. "We will be living on the riverboat?" she fairly squealed.

"Well, any of the vacant apartments that were still standing were snatched up after the earthquake, and we have such good memories of being on the river, I thought it would be fun." He looked to her. "Did I make a mistake?"

She threw her arms around his neck. "It's wonderful! You're wonderful!"

He grinned. "Thank goodness. I was afraid you might not like the idea. I thought perhaps you could set up your business on the first deck until we can rebuild your shop. And on the top deck, we can practice tennis." He chuckled. "But I fear the river will eat most of your hits."

She rolled her eyes, ignoring his teasing, and looped her arm through his and, leaning her head on his shoulder, said, "Have I told you today that you are the most wonderful husband?"

"Compliments from my wife are always

welcome. Now, are you ready to see your new home?" At her kiss of approval, he scooped her up and took her aboard.

WITH THEIR FEW personal items in place, the first item she sat down to stitch was the quilt. She shed many tears as she worked on it, remembering all the happy times she had spent with her father. For the final square, she used the material from the skirt she had been wearing the day of the quake. She had washed it multiple times, but the ashes from the chimney wouldn't come away. She didn't like adding such a stained square to the quilt, but she knew that like life, this quilt would not be as picturesque as she had intended when she had begun to stitch it all those years ago. In the corner, she embroidered, *"He healeth the broken in heart, and bindeth up their wounds. Psalm 147:3."*

Snipping off the end of the thread, she stroked the quilt and looked up at her husband, studying his strong jawline as he read over his work notes, and smiled. "Mr. Clayton, are you ready to go to prison with me?"

Giles crossed the room and swept her into an embrace, bolstering her in strength and courage. "I'll go anywhere, as long as I'm with you."

Grace Hitchcock is the award-winning author of multiple historical novels and novellas, including the American Royalty, Best Laid Plans, and Aprons & Veils series. She holds a Master's in Creative Writing and a Bachelor of Arts in English with a minor in History. Grace lives in South Louisiana with her husband, Dakota, sons, and daughter in a farmhouse that is always filled with the sounds of sweet little footsteps running at full speed. When not writing, chasing her toddlers, or tending to her chickens and golden and labrador retrievers, she's baking something delightful and can usually be found with a book clutched in her fist.

Hearts of Gold

Miss Beaumont's Companion

GRACE HITCHCOCK

CHAPTER ONE

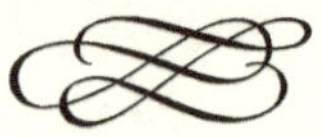

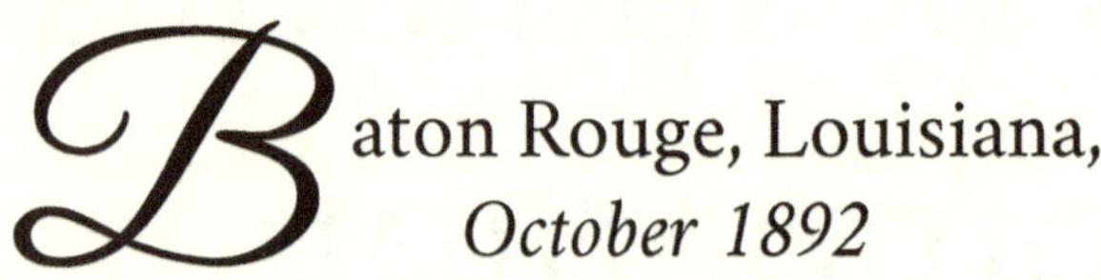

Baton Rouge, Louisiana,
October 1892

"Breathe. Just breathe," Aria whispered as she adjusted the ribbons on her mask, ensuring that her identity was kept safe.

"Now, you know what you must do, Miss St. Angelo," her employer reminded her as the carriage wheels crunched to a halt on the gravel drive in front of the governor's mansion.

"Smile, dance, and make small talk with the politicians." She smoothed the royal-blue replica of a Marie Antoinette gown she was wearing.

"*And* get an introduction with Byron Roderick to secure a call," Mr. Beaumont reiterated. "My daughter is going to pay for disappearing with her aunt this afternoon. Mildred knows how much I need her at Governor Foster's masquerade ball to meet the state senator's son." He turned his dark eyes to her. "If I weren't so concerned about making an inferior impression by being tardy, I would have dragged her back by her coiffure," he growled. "It's imperative for my political future that no one discovers you're not Mildred. If you ruin this night for me, I needn't remind you of the repercussions to your future."

"Yes, sir," she whispered. As the granddaughter of reduced aristocratic Italian immigrants, her options for a respectable living were limited. Even though she cringed at the idea of pretending to be her employer's daughter at the ball, she knew that if she didn't execute this task, Mr. Beaumont would be true to his word and throw her out. She also knew that his daughter could do little to stop it, especially since she was the one who created this ridiculous situation in the first place by sneaking off without a word.

His eyes narrowed at her powdered skin, disguising her olive complexion, and pile of powdered hair. "Straighten your wig. One glimpse of your black hair and the facade is shattered. You're wearing heeled shoes, I hope?"

She nodded. *It's only a little fib. Who will it hurt?* With one hand steadying her wig, Aria gathered her skirts in the other and descended the carriage, stepping into Mildred Beaumont's identity as she crossed the threshold of the governor's mansion. The butler at the door, dressed in Revolutionary-era breeches, coat, and tricornered hat, bowed and removed her cloak. She gave him a small smile of thanks before falling into step behind Mr. Beaumont. At her employer's pointed stare, she realized her blunder and awkwardly threaded her arm through his as if they were truly father and daughter.

Her breath caught at the sight of the

masked ladies and gentlemen on the ballroom floor, whirling in the light of hundreds of candles flickering in the chandeliers, candelabras, and sconces. Some of the gentlemen around her wore pirate trappings, animal heads, and bandit costumes, but most of them merely wore masks. *Probably just to appease their wives,* she surmised by the sullen press of their lips. There were a few women in bold regency gowns, some in Colonial attire, and far too many Marie Antoinette costumes roaming about. She felt a giggle rise within, knowing how furious Mildred would be to know her costly, "unique" costume was donned by at least nine other women. Her exquisite gown had become positively average.

Mr. Beaumont snatched an appetizer from the silver tray of a passing maskless footman who was dressed in the same breeches attire as the butler to distinguish himself from the guests. She reached for a miniature crab cake, but Mr. Beaumont squeezed her elbow.

"Too smelly," he muttered under his

breath as she reluctantly drew back her hand. "Smile brightly and be engaging."

He pulled her toward a group and introduced her to diplomat after senator after representative, making her head dance. She bravely made small talk until her stomach rumbled. Her eyes grew wide as she discreetly pushed a hand against her corset stays and silently begged for the tête-à-tête to end when her stomach rumbled again. Blushing, she quietly excused herself to find the banquet table.

She scanned the room for food but, feeling eyes upon her, turned to see the distinct flash of white-blond hair belonging to Mildred's former beau, Joel Branson, who was staring at her from across the room with his soon-to-be fiancée draped over his arm and the banquet room behind them. Her heart stopped as recognition lit his eyes. She touched the corner of her mask. *Millie must've told him what her gown looked like before he broke their relationship off to be with Fiona,* she thought as he leaned down and whispered into Fiona's ear. Sensing he was about to seek her out, Aria settled for an Italian pastry from one of the dessert tables. Then, before he could make his way through the ballroom, she ducked into an unlit hallway for a bit of privacy. *No wonder Millie decided to escape tonight if she knew that horrid man would be here.* She stepped into the dark recesses of the hallway and stole a bite of cannoli.

BYRON RODERICK HATED the politics behind attending a masquerade ball, but as the son of an influential state senator, he smiled and supported his father as expected. After all, everyone knew he was being groomed for the office himself.

"Don't you think so, Mr. Roderick?" the overeager mother questioned.

"Uh, yes," he replied as he tugged the coat of his costume, hoping his response was the correct answer to the question he hadn't heard. He had attempted to be Paul Revere, but to his amusement, he matched the servants, which was why he'd discarded his mask and put on his wire-rimmed spectacles so he could at least be recognized. But now with the mothers circling him with their single daughters in tow, he began to wish he had left it in place.

Before the current predator could ask yet another question, he excused himself and headed for the dark hallway. *I'll probably pay for that later.* He sighed, rubbing his hands over his eyes as he stepped on something soft and heard a muffled squeal. Startled, he looked down into a pair of dark eyes behind an elaborate Venetian mask. The petite lady, dressed in a cloud of royal blue, stumbled away from his boot and back into a column.

"I'm so sorry, miss!" He grabbed her by the elbows to steady her, spying a half-eaten cannoli in her hand.

"No, it's my fault." She held her hand over her mouth as she talked around a mouthful of pastry, quickly swallowing. "How could you expect to see me in such a dark space?"

"Were you hiding from someone too?" he asked, adjusting his glasses.

Laughing, she nodded and lifted up her

dessert plate. "I haven't had a bite to eat all evening. I was trying to consume this before my, uh, father finds that last politician he wants me to meet. A Mr. Byron Roderick. Have you met him? He's probably just another overweight, red-faced man twenty years my senior." She glanced at the pastry, obviously wishing to finish the treat.

"Ah, I believe I might know whom you are speaking of." He struggled to swallow back his amusement at her candor as he motioned for her to continue eating. "Tell me, what would you rather be doing on a night like this?"

She leaned forward in a conspiratorial whisper. "Honestly? I'd like to finish my book tonight, but my father insisted I go husband hunting instead."

Biting back his laughter at this refreshing young lady, Byron smiled, and with a flourished bow, introduced himself as she took another mouthful.

ARIA CHOKED ON HER PASTRY, and the man dressed in the servant's costume gently slapped her on the back. "I am so sorry," she croaked into her napkin. "I thought you were one of the staff as you weren't wearing a mask! I never would have spoken so outrageously if I thought—"

He laughed, taking her empty plate and setting it aside on a vacant chair. "But then I wouldn't have gotten to know you quite so well, now would I, Miss. . . ?"

"Beaumont." She dipped into a curtsy. "Millie, I mean, Mildred Beaumont," she added in a fuller southern lilt, as Millie might. *How do I fix this? If Mr. Beaumont finds out I've insulted the very man he wishes Millie to marry, he will relieve me of my position.* "So, who were you attempting to run away from?" She took in his towering height, broad shoulders, and chestnut hair and gave him what she hoped was a captivating smile.

"A horde of mothers and their single daughters." He peeked around the column. "But as they seem to be occupied at present, it may be safe to reappear." He turned back to her, extending his hand. "Miss Beaumont, would you do this lawyer the honor of being his partner for the next dance even if he isn't a politician twenty years your senior?"

Feeling her cheeks burn, she let out a shaky laugh as she surrendered her hand to him and then realized that the next dance was still a few minutes away from beginning. Yet, he didn't seem to mind having her hand threaded through his arm.

"So, tell me. What do you like to read when you're not husband hunting?"

She stumbled to answer as Millie would. All she could remember Millie reading was the latest fashion magazines, but as that hardly seemed like a good enough answer to incline his interest to calling, she answered truthfully as herself. "Charles Dickens. My favorite of his works is *Little Dorrit*."

Mr. Roderick's brows rose, and he began another line of questioning that sent her scrambling for Millie-approved answers when the music concluded. *Thank goodness the dance is starting.* She held back a sigh, grateful to be free from fibbing for the moment. Over the next few minutes, she learned that he was an excellent dance partner, and as she dearly loved a waltz but rarely had the opportunity to dance, she allowed herself to get lost in the dips of the violins as he guided her about the room and she hummed along with the music.

"You sing," he stated rather than asked.

She nodded. "My mother is quite accomplished and taught me as a small child."

"Is Mrs. Beaumont with you this evening?"

Realizing her blunder a little too late, she cringed. "I mean *was* accomplished. She still seems so near," she lied, thinking how her perfectly healthy mother was living with their large family in the French Quarter where her father worked as a clerk.

"I'm so sorry to hear that," he replied, mistaking her expression for grief.

Aria dipped her head as she imagined Mildred might. "Thank you."

"May I cut in?"

Aria snapped her head up to find her gaze met by Joel Branson's.

Mr. Roderick bowed to her, giving her

an apologetic smile as Joel stepped in, placing his hand about her waist. "You've become quite slim," he commented.

Aria's eyes flared at the inappropriate comment, but she knew if she answered, he would guess her secret.

"I suppose you're still angry with me for breaking things off with you and forming an attachment with Fiona?"

Not daring to reply, she shook her head.

"Then why have you been avoiding me?" Joel whispered. "I know you want me. You know I only started courting Fiona to show your father I was serious about the dowry's importance. I still love you. All you have to do is convince your father to give you a larger dowry, enough to tempt me away from Fiona's fortune."

She kept her gaze averted as anger rippled through her veins. *Is this what poor Millie had to endure? She said Joel was manipulative, but to use her love for him as a means to obtain wealth? Despicable.*

"Do you really want to take a chance with one of these ancient bachelors or widowers when you know I would adore you as my wife?" He twirled her in his arms as the final notes played. "You have one month before I ask for Fiona's hand. Think carefully, my dear," he whispered as he bowed and left her on the floor, alone.

Mr. Roderick returned to her side, concerned lines etched between his eyes as he escorted her off the floor. "I'm sorry. If I had known you didn't wish to dance with him, I wouldn't have allowed him to cut in."

She shook her head and tried to return a smile to her face. "I didn't know I had let my feelings show so. I was a little uncomfortable, yes, but thankfully it was only for a moment." *Flirt with him.* She turned a sparkling smile up to him. "And now I'm back with you and perfectly content."

He stopped by the refreshment table. Handing her a glass of lemonade, he said, "This may be a bit presumptuous, but I would love to see you again. Would you allow me to call on you tomorrow?"

Her heart skipped a beat at the thought of spending more time with him, but then sank as she realized he wouldn't actually be calling on *her*. Mr. Roderick would be seeing Millie, the youngest daughter of a politician. . .someone of status, not a poor immigrant with weak ties to Italian royalty. She took a quick sip and gave him a bold wink. “As long as it doesn’t interfere with my reading, that would be marvelous.”

This forbidden romance continues in Book Two of the Hearts of Gold series, *Miss Beaumont’s Companion* by Grace Hitchcock.

Sign Up for Grace's Newsletter!

Keep up to date with Grace's news on book releases and giveaways by signing up for her email list at GraceHitchcock.com

FREE from Grace Hitchcock

New Orleans, 1895

Colette Olivier, a young widow who married out of obligation, finds herself at the end of her mourning period and besieged with suitors out for her inheritance. With her pick of any man, she is drawn to an unlikely choice.

The Widow of St. Charles Avenue by Grace Hitchcock
a Second Chance Brides Novella
GraceHitchcock.com

Scan to Claim Your FREE Novella

More in your favorite series . . .

With a hope for belonging, Belle Parish leaves her position as a maid in Charleston to travel to New Mexico to become a mail-order bride. Colt Lawson's letters hold great promise, but something does not add up. Belle flees straight into the Castañeda Hotel Harvey House. Giving up the prospect of marrying, she focuses on her role as a Harvey Girl waitress until a strong Texas Ranger rides into her life.

The Pursuit of Miss Parish by Grace Hitchcock
Aprons & Veils #2
A Mail-Order Bride RomCom

Of all the dares Lorna Elliot had accepted, becoming a Harvey Girl waitress was by far the dumbest. And she had done it to herself in a fit of pique over a Texas Ranger who was mooning over another woman, but now that Ranger Reid is the new sheriff in her hometown, it's going to be impossible for her to move on unless she takes control of her heart—for better, or for worse.

The Enchanting of Miss Elliot by Grace Hitchcock
Aprons & Veils #3
A Friends-to-Lovers RomCom

Tanner Sterling has hunted his last bounty. As a new foreman, he wasn't expecting to rescue a sweet Harvey Girl from a raging river his first day. But, when he sees her on a wanted poster, he knows hunters will be coming for her. Despite wanting to hang up his past along with his gun belt, Tanner will do anything to protect her from the coming storm . . . even if he has to claim the bounty himself.

The Vanishing of Miss Victoria by Grace Hitchcock
Aprons & Veils #4
An Enemies-to-Lovers RomCom

www.ingramcontent.com/pod-product-compliance
Lightning Source LLC
LaVergne TN
LVHW090947080826
845145LV00003B/919

* 9 7 8 1 9 7 0 6 7 5 0 7 8 *